BLACKCOAT

STEVE J. MCHUGH

BLACKCOAT

by

Steve J. McHugh

Copyright © 2021 Steve McHugh This is a work of fiction. Names, characters, organizations, places, events, and incidents are either products of the author's imagination or are used fictitiously. Any resemblance to actual persons, living or dead, or actual events is purely coincidental. Text copyright © 2021 by Steve McHugh

All rights reserved.

No part of this book may be reproduced, or stored in a retrieval system, or transmitted in any form or by any means, electronic, mechanical, photocopying, recording, or otherwise, without express written permission of the publisher.

Published by Hidden Realms Publishing
Cover illustration by SabreCore23-ArtStudioChapter One

To everyone who has supported me over the years.
Thank you.

Also By Steve McHugh

The Hellequin Chronicles

Crimes Against Magic
Born of Hatred
With Silent Screams
Prison of Hope
Lies Ripped Open
Promise of Wrath
Scorched Shadows
Infamous Reign
Frozen Rage

The Avalon Chronicles

A Glimmer of Hope
A Flicker of Steel
A Thunder of War
Hunted

The Rebellion Chronicles

Sorcery Reborn
Death Unleashed
Horsemen's War

Contents

Title Page
Copyright
Dedication
Chapter One
Chapter Two
Chapter Three
Chapter Four
Chapter Five
Chapter Six
Chapter Seven
Chapter Eight
Chapter Nine
Chapter Ten
Chapter Eleven
Acknowledgement

CHAPTER ONE

My cell was little more than a steel framed bed that had seen better days, a mattress that was thin enough that I could feel the springs underneath, and a bucket. I had no idea how long I'd been a prisoner. A few days, probably. There were no windows. No glimpses into the outside world. Just a steady stream of cold air flowing around the badly fit steel door.

I would remain in my dingy cell until those who put me here decided when to execute me. That had been made clear from the moment I'd arrived. That was my fate. A fate I was still trying to figure out how to ensure didn't come to pass.

No matter that I'd worked for the city of Euria—the largest city on the planet of Xolea—and the people who lived there for a decade. No matter that I'd fought against the criminal gangs of Euria while the galaxy around us burned in civil war. No matter that I protected the people of Euria from those same gangs, or that I saw friends give their lives in their duty as judges and Blackcoats of this fine city. No one will ever know that I tried to do the right thing, no one will remember that I stood up against corruption. It was all for nothing.

The realisation had taken a toll on my confidence of being able to get out of the predicament I found myself in.

Xolea is on the far edge of Union space, and consisted of four continent-sized cities. Only Euria, with its population of over twenty million, was considered helpful to the Union in any meaningful way. It was one of the largest manufacturing cities within the entire Union, and during the civil war had been heavily guarded by the Union's fleet to ensure it couldn't be captured or destroyed. Life had been hard in Euria before the war, but during it, when everything was done for *the war effort,* life had gone from hard to almost unbearable, while those in charge got rich and powerful. Richer and more powerful.

Now that the war was over, those who had benefited from it the most refused to give up their gains. Refused to allow people to go back to what had gone before. The gangs that had been around for my entire life, had been taken over by the most affluent in society to be used for their own goals. Keep the people down. Make sure no one tries to stop them from becoming more powerful. I knew the Blackcoats had been infiltrated, knew there was corruption, but I hadn't realised just how deep and far-reaching it had become. Until one dark night on my way home from work, I was jumped by half a dozen people who were meant to be colleagues. Meant to be friends.

The anger at what had been done to me and my city had been all that had sustained me for my time in my dark cell. My partner had vanished, presumed killed by the gangs, and I had been framed for treason against the Union. All because I didn't take bribes. Because I thought that Blackcoats—the Union's law enforcement—were meant to be better than that.

The door to my cell opened with a shriek of metal on stone, bringing with it a gust of freezing air. A Sanctioner stepped inside. One of the five judge ranks. Sanctioners usually didn't deal with crimes that involved the death penalty. I got the feeling in this case there might be an exception.

Two guards—both wearing charcoal-coloured, thick, thermal protection suits, and carrying plasma rifles—stood at the door. Masks covered the lower parts of their face, and each wore dark glasses either to protect their eyes from the harsh sunlight outside or because they thought they looked menacing. Their pale foreheads were all the skin that showed, and both had short, dark hair cut close to the head. The Sanctioner waved them away after one of them brought the man a metal chair that had seen better days. The folds of the Sanctioner's fur-lined, ornate red and yellow robes almost enveloped the chair when he sat.

A scan mask hovered into the room, its two red eyes glowing

inside the dark face. At some point, someone—possibly a psychopath— had decided to make vid recorders look like black face masks with red glowing eyes. I'd always hated them. Not because they were particularly creepy or unpleasant—although they were definitely both—but because I found them to be intrusive. Which, I had to concede, was probably the point.

"Celine Moro," the Sanctioner said, looking down at the brightly lit screen of the data-slate in his hands. "Thirty-eight, female, no family. If you like, I can read you the list of commendations you've received over your career as a Blackcoat? It's honestly very impressive."

I glared at the Sanctioner. "I didn't expect to see you," I said through gritted teeth. "Not here. Not with these murderers and thieves, Gorat."

Gorat took a deep breath and let it out slowly, reclining as much as possible in the rigid chair. "You should have taken the money," he said eventually.

I wanted to rip his tongue out for that. I wanted to beat his head against the thick walls of my cage, but instead I remained seated and seethed inside. "I am a Blackcoat of the district of Euria," I said, keeping my tone level. "I do not accept bribes. It's quite literally a line you have to say when you're sworn in. I'm pretty sure there's an identical line for judges when they're sworn in too."

"Maybe you should have just taken that line as a suggestion," Gorat said with a slight sigh.

"I can't let people's lives be ruined when I could do something to try and stop it," I snapped, before reining in my temper.

"And that, dear Celine, is why you're here in this shithole," Gorat said. "The mask is here to document this conversation for... prosperity. You were offered wealth to look the other way in the dealings of one Trias Nateria, a well-known and wealthy Confessor of the Golden Dawn, and a Councillor of the Union. Did you really think you were going to win this? Did you really think your actions would do anything but end with you here?"

I turned to the scan mask. "You can fly into a wall."

"That's not very mature," Gorat said.

"No, but you're going to execute me anyway because I'm not corrupt. Unlike you, unlike half of the people I worked with." The words tumbled free before I could stop them. "I did what was right and for that I end up here. I end up a criminal. Framed for treason because I was an inconvenience. Because I wasn't corrupt. Framed by a Councillor of the Union. Godsdamned it, Gorat, these people aren't meant to be tyrants, that's why The Wardens exists."

"There are no Wardens on Euria," Gorat said.

"Which is exactly why people like Trias are allowed to do whatever they like." I wanted to throw something at the wall in frustration.

The Wardens were responsible for the protection of every single Councillor and their families throughout the Union. But they also investigated any wrongdoing by those same Councillors. If they'd been on Euria there was a good chance I wouldn't have been stuck in a damn cell, and Trias wouldn't have been allowed to make himself the tyrant of the city.

"You always were too stubborn, too sure of what was right and wrong," Gorat said, angry. "Everyone else just manages. You don't have to like it, but it's how things are done here. Especially during the war."

"The war has been over for two years."

"Yes, which is why we need to help the people of this planet,' Gorat explained slowly, as if I was an idiot.

"And corruption helps them, how?"

"The workers here need these drugs, need to be helped."

"Because they got addicted helping the war effort," I said, the anger bubbling up inside me once again.

"There's no going back now," Gorat said. "Too many people made too much money to change things back to how they were."

"Then maybe those things *need* to change," I snapped.

"You think you're the one to do it?" Gorat snapped back. "Trias doesn't play games. He wants you dead. He wants to know what you know, and then he's going to have you executed, and your body will be taken to one of the factories and burned up in a furnace. The people will look the other way, and do you know why? Because Trias either pays them to, or they're not worth his money and they're so terrified of him that they do it for free."

"He's a Confessor of the Golden Dawn and a Councillor of the Union," I said, not really sure how to convey the betrayal I felt, not only at Gorat and my old comrades turning against me, but that a Confessor—a man who was meant to protect the people of their planet—could turn his back on everything he was meant to believe in. For profit and power. The fact he was a Councillor too, made the transgression doubly hard to take. Two jobs that were meant to be carried out by those who were meant to want the best for their people. It was a corruption of two great institutes of the Union, and when I'd first discovered the truth, it had made me physically ill.

Gorat sighed again.

"You knew my parents," I said, my voice now barely above a whisper. "You worked with them. You knew me as a child, and now you're going to be the one to have me executed. Why keep me here for however long it's been? Why not just kill me?"

"I told you, Trias needs to know what you told to whom."

"So you can go and kill more people?"

"Your parents were good people in a different time," Gorat said, rubbing his eyes after several seconds of silence. "They would have taken the bribe."

I *really* wanted to hit him for that.

"Trias wanted to come see you himself," Gorat continued. "That's why no one has hurt you yet. But instead, he's decided you aren't worth him venturing out into the cold. You're just not important enough to him."

"I could have brought him down," I said more to myself than Gorat.

"You gathered more information on his operation than anyone else ever has. You and that other Blackcoat you were working with."

"His name was Prasan," I said, the familiar and warming sensation of anger keeping me from breaking down.

"He's dead by the way," Gorat said. "They'd considered framing you for the murder, but honestly, you both vanishing is much easier. Neither of you have families, both single, both married to the job, both disposable."

"He didn't deserve that," I said. Prasan did have a family, a sister. They'd kept their mutual existence secret from those they worked with. Prasan the Blackcoat, and Rika the criminal arms-dealer. Having a criminal or a Blackcoat as family members didn't inspire confidence or trust in their allies. "He was a good Blackcoat. He was a good man."

"He was," Gorat said. "I made sure his death was quick. It was all I could do for him. Some of Trias' more… ardent supporters wanted him flayed. Wanted to send a message to other Blackcoats, but I managed to convince them otherwise."

"Am I meant to be grateful?" I shouted.

"You're meant to understand that I can only do so much for you and those you work with," Gorat said. "I can't begin to tell you what some of those same people wanted to do to you. I got Trias to agree that making you vanish without a trace was better in the long term, but if you won't tell me who you spoke to, his people are going to get to make you talk. I can't stop that."

"So, did you come in here to get information, or to taunt me?"

"This isn't easy for me either," Gorat said.

"Oh, I'm sorry, are you being betrayed by your own people and about to be executed for standing up against a crime boss?" I looked around the room. "No? Just me then."

"Councillor, not crime boss," Gorat corrected, his tone soft as if imparting a lesson.

I laughed in his face. "If it walks like a crime boss, talks like a crime boss, and shoots people in the face like a crime boss, he's a crime boss."

"This isn't going to get us anywhere, is it?" Gorat said with a sigh. He got to his feet and looked down on me as if about to scold a child. "For the final time, Trias told me that if you cooperated, your death would be quick. But if not, then the guards will come in here and get the information out of you in another, much less pleasant way."

"They're going to sing a song?" I asked. "Or maybe do a dance routine? I think both of those would be less pleasant."

"You never could keep a civil tongue in your head," Gorat said, disapprovingly.

"And, apparently, you never could stop taking bribes to look the other way," I said, leaning back on my bed. "I guess we've both been disappointed today."

I looked up at the mask as it stared at me with its red eyes. "Trias, when you read this back, or watch the vid, or whatever you're going to do, I hope you realise one day someone will actually find you in that lovely home of yours looking down over the rest of the district, and they'll kill you. I'm just sorry to say I won't be there to celebrate it myself."

"Trias controls this city," Gorat said, the palm of his hand against the door. "You should have realised that. Soon, the four guards in this building will come for you. They will take you to the room where you will eventually meet your death."

"Only four?" I asked.

"Torture doesn't take many people," Gorat said. "They will hurt you before you die. You could have ensured that didn't happen."

"*You* could have ensured that didn't happen," I said, throwing his own words back at him.

"Goodbye, Celine," Gorat said, pushing open the door, letting in the cold air from outside.

The mask left the cell first and Gorat reached inside his robes and placed a small box on the floor. The rectangular box was eight inches long by three inches wide, and was no deeper than the length of my finger. It was coloured orange and red with yellow trim, and reminded me of Gorat's robe.

"Goodbye," Gorat said again, and left me alone in my cell.

I stared at the box for some time. I wasn't really sure what to do with it. Was it a bomb? No, probably not. That seemed too much like hard work for Gorat. My curiosity eventually overrode my feelings of trepidation and concern, and I picked up the box, flicking open the metal clasp and lifting the lid.

Inside sat a six-inch-long carbonate-fibre combat knife. I lifted it free and examined it. It was light, and sharpened to a dangerous edge. Knives were used by anyone from generals to street scum, but carbonate-fibre was different. They were used to by Special Forces members to be able to cut through shields and armour. It was the same material used to make the battleships and was almost indestructible against conventional weapons. It was the weapon of an assassin, of a warrior. And they were banned on Euria for one reason and one reason only: Trias and his loyal supports wore specially designed force shields at all times. If you wanted to kill one of them, you'd need to get close, and there was little chance of that with all of their guards and spies looking out for them.

Thankfully the carbonate blade would work just as well on flesh as it would on those with shields. The question was why had Gorat left it? Had he intended for me to use it to escape, did he think I could use it to kill Trias? Or had he left it because he knew I would try to escape and would be killed in the process. Giving me a heroic death instead of one screaming through hours of torture? Did it matter? Probably not. But it still played on my mind. Whatever else happened, escaping from the cell was my first move.

The shuffling of feet sounded outside the cell, and I held the knife down by my leg, the blade against the outside of my thigh, hidden from the man in foul weather gear who opened the door and stepped inside.

"It's time to go," he said with a snarl, a plasma rifle casually slung over one shoulder. He considered me no threat. He was an idiot.

"I think I'm okay right here," I told him.

"I didn't say I was giving you a choice," he barked, stepping toward me, reaching for my arm. I sprung toward him, brushing his arm aside as he tried to grab me. He never saw the dagger until it was buried in his throat, his eyes wide with shock. He was dead a moment later.

I stepped aside as I removed the dagger, avoiding any blood

as the guard collapsed forward. I dragged him further into my cell and checked the hallway beyond, finding it empty. There were three more guards somewhere in the building I'd been held in, and I had to work fast in case they were on the way to me as well.

I removed his red, fur-lined jacket and put it on; it was a little big, but it was that or deal with the sub-zero temperatures of a Euria winter without one, and that wasn't much of a choice at all. I removed his second layer of clothing too—a skin-tight, black, cold-resistant top that was designed to change size to fit any frame. Anything to make sure I didn't freeze to death the moment I stepped outside. I took his back holster and the energy pistol inside it, leaving the well-used plasma rifle where it was. The damn things only take six to eight shots before the magazine overheats and you need a new one. An energy pistol can put three times that number of shots out.

It took me a few minutes to get dressed, and every noise outside of the cell made me pause, and pick up a weapon, waiting for the inevitable attack. But none came. I wondered where the other guards were. Had they expected this one guard to be able to deal with me? Were they torturing some other poor soul? I pushed the thoughts aside; I didn't need the distraction right now. I was soon dressed and ready to battle both the enemy inside the facility, and the elements outside.

I picked up the cell key card—a small, transparent blue device — and after checking the hallway once again—and finding it thankfully empty—I stepped out of the cell. The cold air whipped through the hallway of the building. Six doors ran the length of one side of the hallway, and large windows opposite each showcased the frozen tundra outside, the snow coming down hard. There would be several feet in a few hours in some parts, a dangerous time of the year for those working on the trams moving goods to and from the space port.

A light overhead flickered, and I counted to thirty to see if anyone would come check on their friend. But after forty-five seconds, I decided it was safe to continue.

I had no idea exactly where I was or why Gorat had left me

a weapon, but I planned on finding out. And then I was going to find Trias and we were going to have a long conversation about the error of his ways.

CHAPTER TWO

The warehouse had four guards. That's what Gorat had told me. With one dead in my cell, only three stood between me and freedom. Or at least a chance to become free. To bring justice down on those who had conspired with Trias. To bring down Trias himself. Preferably from a great height.

I paused. Not sure how I was going to bring Trias down. Getting out of the warehouse was step one, but if I didn't have a step two, I wasn't going to last the day. With a deep, calming breath a plan began to formulate in my mind. It was only the barest bones of an idea, but it was better than nothing, and it gave me hope that I might actually come out of this with my life. Or at least with the knowledge that Trias was going to be having as bad of a day as I was.

In a semi-crouch, I set off again along the hallway, my carbonate knife in one hand and energy pistol in the other. I paused at each of the cell doors, not wanting any surprises. Three cells in I found the first inhabited cell. I used the key card against the electronic locks on the door and pulled it open. Inside was an old man who had been dead for some time, his body frozen solid under the thin blanket that had been pulled up to his chin.

"I'm sorry," I whispered and left the cell, continuing along and finding the next cell occupied too.

The door unlocked and it squealed as it opened. Inside was a semi-conscious woman of about thirty. She was covered in a thick fur-lined coat, and appeared to be coming through some kind of drug-induced haze, but I didn't have time to do more for her. I left the cell door ajar—not open enough to let the freezing air seep in

—and hoped she'd be able to get out of the warehouse in one piece.

Four shots echoed in the distance before I reached the end of the cell block hallway. I paused, unsure whether to go toward the shots or try to figure out how to get around them and head outside. Unfortunately, I didn't know whereabout in the city I was. I could step outside in the middle of what appeared to be fast becoming a blizzard and still have no idea where I was. And then I'd be dead.

Euria was a city that rarely slept, and was made up of dozens of smaller districts. A lot of items came through the large warehouse centre of the district before moving on to other parts of Euria. Our district was like the sorting office of the entire southeast of the city. It was home to vast amounts of wealth, and the people who ran the warehouses and factories lived in one of four towering Spires that sat at the far east of the district, so that the owners who lived in their sprawling penthouses within could look out over the frozen tundra toward the mountain ranges. The rich person's playground was how I'd once heard it described, and it was a fair comparison. Some said they were the only people who ever saw through the perma-fog that blanketed the district when winter really set in; I wasn't sure if I believed that.

The poor though, they didn't do so well. They worked hard in the factories and warehouses, living there and rarely ever going outside. Towering apartment blocks had underground trams linked them to the factories. For months at a time, the workers of the city rarely stepped outside unless they were properly protected, or a driver of one of the large trucks. Or they wanted to end it all. The spring brought the thaw, and with it, the reveal of those who had decided to end their lives on their own terms.

If I was in one of the warehouses, that meant that I would have to pass through the poorer district to get to my own residential block. On the plus side, that meant I could probably navigate around the larger factories and avoid the tens of thousands of people who worked there. Winter hadn't quite set in, so I could use the above ground with little concern of actually meeting people as more and more workers took to the trams.

On the minus, it meant that if I *was* seen out in the open by anyone, they might consider me someone unsavoury and react accordingly. My residential block was closer to the Spires than the slums and factories, but that didn't mean I lived a life of anything close to luxury.

If I was honest with myself, I should run. I should run as far as my legs would take me, but Trias had destroyed my life. He'd murdered my friend, he'd had me kidnapped by people I thought were my friends, and he was going to have me tortured, executed, disposed of.

Trias owned too many, held too much power for me to be allowed out of the district. My life was never going to be what it was, and now my options were hide in the district and hope I never get discovered, which wasn't really my kind of choice, or take the fight to Trias. I liked that idea a whole lot more.

Either way, I needed intel. I needed to find my kidnappers, and I needed them to talk. If they thought that my day was bad, theirs was about to get a whole lot worse.

At the end of the hallway was the choice between an ascending staircase and set of ajar metal double doors that had been painted with yellow graffiti that had worn off over time, leaving whatever message the artist had attempted an unreadable mess. I stood at the bottom of the staircase, the steps were old, the dark wood rotten in places. I doubted anyone would have taken the stairs unless they had no other choice, I wasn't even sure it would support the weight of anything more than a few rats.

I moved to the double doors and waited, listening out for anything or anyone beyond. When I was all but certain it was safe, I eased open one of the doors a little more and peered inside. It was a large hall, at least sixty feet in length with wooden floors in a similar state to the staircase. Metal sheets had been placed between the exposed beams of the floor, giving a safe path through what would have otherwise been a dangerous journey. I peered into the first large hole I came across but couldn't even tell how deep the drop would be to the basement below.

I moved slowly across the hall, not wanting my steps to echo over the metal, more than through a fear of falling. An identical set of double doors sat at the opposite end, the graffiti on that wall in bright red: *watch your step.*

No kidding, I thought to myself with as much sarcasm as I could muster.

It took me some time to reach the exit, but after making sure there was no one waiting behind them, I slipped through the doors to... another hallway. This whole place was just a maze of halls and corridors. My heart sank as I wondered just how long it was going to take to find a way out.

Three bodies were slumped on the ground to one side of the hallway. The blood was fresh. The recipients of the gunshots I'd heard earlier. All three wore old, tatty clothes. All looked like they hadn't bathed in some time. Two men, one woman. I couldn't have given even a rough idea of their ages due to the amount of damage done to their faces with the gunshots, but all three had long, greying hair. None wore coats, and had on sleeveless tops, revealing the track marks in their arms and wrists.

Energy Mist. A drug that had been brought in during the civil war. It let people work longer hours, go longer without needing to sleep or eat. Take enough of it, and it let people go through work without even thinking, working only on muscle memory or something like it. Take too much of it, and it destroyed you from the inside out. Rotted your organs, turned your blood into a thick black syrup and, eventually, turned you into... well, there wasn't an official name for it. The Blackcoats called them *the murk* because if you took enough of it you turned into something... else. You killed over nothing, bludgeoned your own parents to death for the slightest indiscretion. You no longer cared about anything but your own need to hurt everyone around you. Pain in others became your catharsis. I'd put down dozens of people on it. People who had once been productive members of society, now practically bathing in the blood of their once friends.

And it had made Trias richer and more powerful than he could have ever been without it. It killed thousands of people, tens of thousands, but they were the poor. Workers. People who didn't matter to the rich. What do they care about a few workers when there are thousands to take their place? The very notion of it boiled my blood, and seeing those three humans cast aside and murdered in a hellhole, made me want to hurt someone.

The end of the hallway was yet another metal door—this one without graffiti—and as I stopped outside of it, I wondered if I was about to find dead kidnappers or more victims of Trias who had been put to death. Or worse, a murk looking for a fix.

The cold from outside seeped into the warehouse the further I made my way through, as the building was well past dilapidated, and appeared to serve only as a place for Trias to have people tortured and, or, killed.

I pushed open the door slightly and peered into a large open foyer. The double doors to the building were not quite shut, and snow had piled up just inside.

Three dead men sat on seats around a make-shift table where they'd been playing a card game that was popular with the workers of the district. Gambling was illegal in the district, but like anywhere, illegal just meant keep out of sight of anyone who might arrest you for it.

Gorat sat in a chair that had seen better days. The scan mask lay on the ground, a hole where one of its red eyes had been.

"You did this?" I asked, stepping into the room and noticing the blood stains that covered all three of the dead criminals.

Gorat nodded, and placed an suppressed energy pistol on the table, scattering the cards over the side onto the floor. "I'm not sure why."

"Not much of an answer," I said. I didn't feel like being charitable. Gorat might have helped me escape, but he was also working for the people who had put me in the cell in the first place.

"I know that I have long since lost any moral authority, but I just told myself that one day I would be able to repent. That as bad as I was, at least I wasn't Trias with his holier than thou attitude and corrupt soul. But I am as bad. I saw that the moment you were taken. I saw what you'd tried to achieve, and I told myself that it was your fault for being so damned pig-headed. I was sat here, listening to these men laugh about killing, and about how much they enjoyed getting to kill people like you, people who thought they could fight back. And I couldn't listen anymore."

"You murdered them because you grew a conscience?" I asked with a slight chuckle. I didn't find it funny, but it was that or punch Gorat in his face, and I doubted the latter of those options would do me much good long-term.

"You can't go back to your own life," Gorat said. "Trias has made sure of that. One of them had a communication that told him your residence was destroyed, just in case you had any intel that might harm him or his people. Your neighbours were killed because one happened to see them at your place. Trias is eliminating anyone who might be able to hurt him. Two more Blackcoats have been executed this morning because they made the mistake of saying the wrong thing to the wrong person about your disappearance."

I stood there, numb. "They killed my neighbours because they saw something they shouldn't have?"

Gorat nodded. "They are in the process of completely removing everything about you. As far as the district is concerned, when they've finished, you never existed in the first place. Trias has enough power to arrange that. To make people disappear as if they never existed. He has control over people by being a Councillor and even more control via his church. No one should have that much power over the people they're meant to serve, but he doesn't care, and I doubt he's going to slow down now. The fact that he could just have someone's accomplishments deleted, their name banned from the lips of those who used to know them, it's too much."

"I'm going to kill him," I said. I hadn't been sure of it until that moment, but now I was. Trias had to die.

Gorat laughed. "How? You can't even get into the Spire he lives in. You certainly can't get to the penthouse. Hells, I can't even imagine you'd be able to make it a day outside of here once his people start looking for you. He's too powerful."

"How do I get into the Spire?"

"You're going to need weapons, armour, equipment," Gorat said as if I hadn't spoken at all.

I picked up the scan mask and smashed it onto the table, getting Gorat's attention. "How do I get into the Spire?" I asked again, slower this time.

"You can't," he said. "There are too many guards, too many people who will see you."

I looked out of the nearest window. The Spire was a blip in the distance, but there had to be a way. I couldn't get to it from above, that was out. I couldn't get to it from another building, so that was out too. And apparently, I couldn't get to it from just walking through the front door.

I tried to figure out some way I could get to Trias without having to get killed before I'd even gotten close. "I need military equipment," I said. "Any way to get some?"

"In Euria?" Gorat asked. "Not unless you get it via less than legal means."

"There are black-market dealers who work out of the underground slums," I said, mostly to myself.

"You're really going to go ahead with this idea?" Gorat asked. "They'll kill you."

"Then I'll die on my feet," I snapped.

I walked past Gorat, and picked up a large, heated cloak from the floor that only had small splashes of blood on it. I wrapped it around my shoulders, activating it and waiting for a few seconds for it to actually start working. When I was satisfied I wasn't about to freeze to death the second I stepped out of the building, I removed a hip holster from one of the dead criminals and exchanged it for the back holster I'd taken from the man I'd killed outside my cell. I placed my energy pistol inside the holster and tested it to make sure it didn't snag. I picked up a heat mask and a pair of fur-lined black gloves from one of the dead. The gloves fit perfectly, and the mask had an almost new filter in it, although I picked up a few more from the pockets of the criminals who no longer needed them.

When satisfied I was as prepared as I was ever going to be, I grabbed a few more magazine packs from the dead men, as well as a compass that sat on one of their wrists. They weren't going to be using them.

I turned back to Gorat, who remained in his seat. "I assume you'll be staying here," I said, unable to keep the anger from my tone.

"I'm a dead man already," he said. "No point in letting Trias torture me."

"He was going to have these assholes do that to me," I snapped.

"If he catches you, you will not die for a long time," Gorat said. "He'll make sure of it. He'll make you into a cautionary tale about what happens to people who cross him. It's what he's going to do to me once he figures out I helped you escape. I don't have family for him to kill though, so I guess the joke's on him."

I walked to the door and pulled it open, glad for the warmth of my cloak and jacket. I looked back to Gorat who was on his feet, energy pistol in hand and held by his hip. I turned back to him, letting the door swing closed behind me.

"I didn't do this for you," Gorat said. "I did it for me."

"You sure you want to do this?" I asked, my hand immediately down by my own energy pistol, my fingers flexing slightly by the holster, ready for whatever Gorat had planned.

"I don't see another way," Gorat said. "I can't kill myself. I just can't."

"You're a coward," I told him. "A coward who should have done the right thing a long time ago. Why help me escape?"

"I don't know," Gorat said. "I think you might be able to stop Trias where I couldn't. I think you might be the only person left who isn't afraid of him, or already working for him. I don't like you, Celine, but I do respect you."

"I don't care about your respect," I told him. "I don't care if you like me."

"That's why I helped you," Gorat said. "That's why I have to do this."

Gorat raised his energy pistol and I drew my own, shooting

him in the eye.

    I re-holstered the weapon, yanked open the door, and stepped out into the frozen district.

CHAPTER THREE

The night in Euria felt more oppressive than usual. Most of the people who lived in the district never actually saw the daylight during the colder months, when it was darker longer, or the sun was hidden behind a thick, frozen fog from the factories. Sometimes, I wondered if it was the same in other parts of the city, if anyone there ever got to look up at the skies above the fog.

The snow fell hard, making moving through the district difficult. No one was outside, thankfully, but it was hard to get my bearings. It wasn't until I saw one of the mega-factories that I knew where I was. The ominous orange glow that the factories caused as their emissions combined with the fog, could be seen in the distance. I was far enough away from them that I had quite the walk ahead of me.

I'd patrolled the factories a thousand times. It was big enough that some of the people there had started to develop a mini culture, separate from the rest of the city. It happened quite often when tens of thousands of people lived and worked in the same place for months and years on end. Most of the time it was something the Blackcoats and people in charge accepted, but there had been occasions when it had needed to be quashed before anything untoward began to take place. Once, a group of people had turned a culture into a blood-cult, and the bodies had started to pile up.

There were half a dozen mega-factories in my district alone, and my superiors were often concerned that what happened in one might spread to the others. The mega-factories were too important, with too much wealth involved to allow anything to happen to them. But with all that wealth and power came corruption. No matter how much we tried to fight it, to stamp it out before it took root, it always managed to claw its way back. Time and time again.

Occasionally items inside the mega-factories went missing. Sometimes it was food, other times it was pieces of machinery, or weapons. One or two things disappearing every few days by one person was bad enough, but when there were thousands of people doing it on a daily basis, it couldn't be ignored.

The black-market was a network of tunnels under the district. They'd been abandoned generations ago when the apartment blocks had been built, and were now homes for criminals, delinquents, and anyone else who wanted to vanish from the watchful eye of those above. A lot of them worked in the factories or at the warehouses, and simply slinked off to their hovels when it became too hard, or they got discovered stealing or breaking some other law they felt didn't apply to them.

Everyone knew where the slums were, and everyone knew there were black-market sales that went on down there. For the most part they were ignored, allowed to continue uninterrupted. Occasionally a criminal would get too big for their boots, or would start to think they were untouchable, and then the Blackcoats and judges would crack down, scattering the criminals and arresting any too slow or stupid to run.

The black-market was an ants' nest under our feet, and one that I'd gone to for help in the past. There was a strange relationship between black-market vendors and the Blackcoats. We let them be, they fed us intel, or gave us untraceable weapons to go after people we didn't want the higher-ups pinging back to us. On this particular occasion, I needed equipment. The black-market vendors shipped things out of the district to other parts of Xolea, to other vendors, and to those who could afford their prices. The more enterprising vendors lived in the slums to avoid us, but they'd made themselves rich from breaking the law. Not rich or powerful enough to be a part of Trias' power circle, I imagine, but rich enough to know that should Trias get his way, those who opposed him in the black-market would be next on his list of targets.

I'd only been walking for a few minutes, my feet occasionally sinking into the increasingly thick snow, when I realised I was lost. The wind had picked up, bringing the fog with it and turning everything into an identical piece of landscape. There were no pieces of architecture or landmarks to figure out where I might be, so I just kept on in what I hoped was a straight line.

There was no need to worry about the trucks during weather this bad—no factory owner would risk a whole shipment by using them when the trams were right there underground. It was slower to load and unload from a tram, but it was a damn sight safer.

I stepped, lost my footing and stumbled, soon finding myself rolling down a hill, picking up speed, until I hit the bottom, continuing to roll for several feet while masses of loose snow followed in my wake. When I looked up at the hill, I couldn't see the top for the fog. I was lucky.

More snow, more no way of knowing where I was. I was going to freeze to death or fall down something a lot less pleasant than a gentle slope if I didn't find my bearings soon.

In the foggy haze, I spotted a looming structure and headed off in that direction. Looming structure mean something that wasn't snow. Whether it was good or bad, I'd figure out later.

The structure was a tall guard post, although it appeared to be unmanned, which meant more luck for me. There was a small glass-covered enclosure, which led to a sixty-foot ladder to a platform above. Usually two guards stood sentinel, at least one with a coil rifle, and watched for anything or anyone causing trouble. There were creatures on Xolea that would tear into the factories and kill people should they be left alone. And some creatures — like the lair rat—would breed so quickly and so dangerously that they could overrun an entire mega-factory and put it out of business for months while the infestation was dealt with.

The guard post was also empty, the door to the ladder locked —something that can't be done when anyone is on top of the post. The weather probably got the guards re-posted elsewhere. Guards usually work alongside the Blackcoats, although there was a mixture of grudging respect, and outright dislike between the two. The Blackcoats thought the guards little more than thugs, and the guards thought the Blackcoats were a little too far up their own backsides. I figured both were probably right.

The terminal in the guard post was operational, and thankfully every guard post had a map and their location right there on the screen.

"A mile east of my destination," I said with a deep sigh. "That's not brilliant." A mile out in the frozen tundra of the city was going to be a long walk, but there was nothing to do except get on with it and try not to die while doing so. It would be an inauspicious end to my attempt at justice—or vengeance, if I was being honest with myself—to freeze to death and not be found until the spring thaw.

From the terminal, I accessed the Blackcoat informant site. The informant site was free to anyone in the district, and was where a lot of people sent tips and information about crimes. It was a useful tool, but it was also the hidden log-in for access to the Blackcoats site.

I stared at the opening page for several seconds. If I tried to log in, and it worked, I'd have maybe ten minutes before the area was swarming with guards and Blackcoats. If it didn't let me in, then I'd have informed those in charge that I was alive for nothing.

Nothing ventured, nothing gained. I tapped 'C' on the word Blackcoat four times, followed by the 'K' twice, taking it to the login page for the Blackcoats. I used the onscreen keyboard to enter my username and password, but my finger hovered over the enter button. I tapped it and held my breath.

The screen thought for a second and then changed to my Blackcoat account. They hadn't gotten around to deleting me yet. That was either an oversight on their part—the tech guys were swamped at the best of times—or I was being set up. Either way, the risk had already been taken.

I flicked through screens, hurrying now that a countdown would have started, and found the access to the city-wide camera network. I typed in the number for my apartment block. The footage from the attack was gone; couldn't have that getting out. However, moving back a few minutes caught the same group of Blackcoats entering my apartment building. Nothing unusual about that. I zoomed in on the faces of the three men, committing them to memory, and then settled on the face of a woman who was meant to be my friend: Ekhar Sard.

Ekhar was a few inches taller than my own five-foot-ten, but we had similar athletic builds. Where my hair was short and dark brown, hers was long and dark red. Unlike me, she'd been a guard and worked her way up to Blackcoat. We'd worked together for four years. I'd met her husband. She was a hell of an investigator, and someone I thought I could trust. Ekhar had been the first one to hit me after I'd been subdued while I slept. I remembered the pain in my jaw, her kick to my ribs as I lay defenceless, the laughter of the men she'd been with.

Before I became a Blackcoat, I worked for the Union military. It was expunded from my record, so officially, I was just in another part of the planet on a joint operations task force with guard members. In reality, I was off-world doing things that still gave me nightmares. Blackcoats are highly trained, considered by many to be the elite law enforcement branch of the entire Union. They thought they were the biggest threat in Euria. But they were wrong.

Given the chance, I was going to find Ekhar, and I was going to kill her, too. Her and those who had helped abduct me.

In my head, three minutes had gone by. I went back to the city-wide camera system and pulled up a classified search for Ekhar. Blackcoats were all tracked via their badge. I didn't have mine, so it was no longer a problem for me, but I was pretty sure that Ekhar would have had hers.

The terminal considered the request for a few moments, before returning a result; Ekhar was in her apartment. Too far out of the way for me to make a stop for a little vengeance. She would have to wait, although I was certain that when they discovered I was still alive, she'd be volunteering to finish the job.

Four minutes.

I took a deep breath and ran a search through my Blackcoat ID for off-world capable transmitters. There'd be one in the Spire, but that was far too dangerous. One in Blackcoat headquarters, but that would also result in me being dead.

The results were still being collated when I heard sirens in the distance. I stopped the search, wiped the history on the terminal then shattered the screen with a shot from my energy pistol. A second shot into the wiring behind it made enough mess to make it look like I was hiding something, hopefully giving me some time before they figured out what I was looking for and gave chase.

I was out of the guard post and running as fast as I dared into the snow, moving east as the sirens grew louder. I stayed alongside a large building, using it for a guide more than anything else. I risked a look back and spotted the flashing red lights in the distance. I was several hundred meters or so away, and the fog made sure I was almost invisible to the eye, but they had body heat scanners and I needed to make sure I wasn't the only thing out here giving off any heat.

I climbed over a partially collapsed fence and dropped into an alleyway between the warehouse I'd been following, and a smaller building. A neon pink sign hung from the wall, declaring it to be a restaurant, casting an eerie glow all around as the light reflected off the snow. The windows were shuttered, although I imagined the interior to be full of workers having come up through the basement levels of the place on break. Most restaurants in the city had long since adapted to the needs of those who worked here.

Steam rose from vents alongside the building, raising the temperature of the entire alleyway by a dozen degrees. The snow here was still a few inches deep, and the steam was definitely fighting a losing battle, but with everything around me being warm, it would be harder for anyone to pick up my heat signature. Hopefully.

I ran along the alleyway, turning right at the end and continuing down what was clearly a street judging from the number of lights that protruded from the ever-increasing mounds of snow. Thankfully, there were no vehicles out, so running across the road and ducking down the first alleyway I came across was easily done.

More sirens caused me to pause and slow to a walk. The long alleyway became increasingly dark and imposing as the buildings on either side loomed over me. The sirens weren't close but I couldn't pinpoint their exact location, so I continued at a walk.

The compass told me I was still heading east, so at least I knew I was going in the right direction, even if I had no idea of knowing exactly *where* I was.

After more alleyways, more streets, and more than one slight panic when the sound of sirens drifted over me, I arrived at a street with a yellow neon arrow pointing to the right. I looked over and spotted a second arrow attached to the side of a large warehouse. It pointed down to an alleyway. I took a deep breath and continued on.

Steam snaked from the half dozen large vents on the side of the alleyways next to the towering warehouse that had long since begun to collapse. If something was no longer needed, it was allowed to crumble. I wondered if that was the same in other parts of the city, or if that was just Trias' influence. I guessed now I'd never find out.

This far to the east of the city was a place the Blackcoats and guards rarely ventured unless they had no choice. The black-market vendors ruled this area, and I wondered if Trias' influence here would cause the person I wanted to see to just hand me over to the man. I hoped not.

At the end of the alleyway, I stood before a metal shutter with a giant orange cross painted on it. I sighed; this was probably not going to be the most fun experience. Blackcoats and black-market vendors might have a symbiotic relationship in many ways, but I was almost certain that my abduction and, or, death would have filtered through by now. If anyone saw me and thought they could make some quick coin, I could find myself in another cell in the not-too-distant future. Thankfully, my hood was pulled up, and the mask that stopped the cold from getting into my face would obscure my identity. At least for a little while.

I banged on the shutter, thankful for the thick gloves. Sirens wailed in the distance, followed by screams not long after. The Blackcoats and judges were out doing their jobs. The weather didn't matter, there were always lawbreakers whose heads needed busting. I wondered how many of them were doing Trias' bidding. I wondered how many of my old comrades would now put a bullet in my head and claim their reward.

The metal shutter pulled up with a sound that went right through me, revealing a large man with a shaved head. He wore winter weather gear that probably cost more than the average factory worker made in a year, and yet he was inside a run-down squaller opening metal shutters. Criminals never were very good at being inconspicuous.

"You are?" he asked, his accent placing him from somewhere outside the district.

"I need to talk to Rika," I said.

"She doesn't take walk-ins," the man said, reaching out to push me away.

I pushed his arm to the side, stepped around him, and smashed my elbow into his floating rib. He roared in pain, and tried to swat me away, but I ducked under his arm, drilling my fist up under his jaw, snapping his head back with enough force to make him stagger. He shook his head but couldn't clear it in time to stop me driving my forearm into his jaw with everything I had. The big man dropped to the ground with a thud and remained unmoving.

"Celine?" Rika asked from just inside the building. She wore a set of black and green winter weather gear that looked like it had been custom made. Her long blue hair—Sarcian hair changed colour from black to blue or yellow depending on how warm they were— fell over her pale green-skinned shoulders. The familiar scar that went from just under her one yellow eye, to above her lip was almost a welcomed sight. Her other eye had long since gone, although I had no idea how and she wasn't the kind of person you asked stupid questions to.

"Your boy didn't play nice," I said, stepping into the building.

Rika clicked her fingers and two more men—both identical in appearance to the unconscious one—dragged their friend inside and closed the shutter.

"I never said you could come in," Rika said.

"I need your help," I told her.

"No," Rika said, turning away.

"Wait." I stepped forward and found the end of a plasma rifle pointing right at my head.

"Why?" Rika asked. "Because we grew up together? Because we know one another? Why should I help you?"

"Because Trias killed your brother."

CHAPTER FOUR

"Prasan is dead?" Rika asked me, her voice wobbling slightly.

She'd taken me through the building to a set of stairs that lead underground. She'd been silent the whole way, and for at least part of it, I was unsure whether she was going to kill me before I ever got the chance to explain what had happened.

I nodded, pretty sure that words wouldn't have made much difference. Glow globes lit the small room we were in, bathing everything in a dim orange. They continued to flicker as Rika hit them more than once; the traditional method of getting technology to work properly.

"I'm going to need more information than that," Rika said, her tone suggesting that I either got on with it or we were about to have an exceptionally large fight.

I told her almost everything I knew.

When I was done, Rika leaned back in her chair, closed her one eye, and let out a long sigh. "You're going to kill Trias," she said eye still closed.

"That's the plan."

"You don't just want to run? A lot of people would run."

"He'll find me," I told her as I leaned up against what looked like an old pile of junk. "He'd kill anyone I was with too. I can't risk it. Once Trias is dead, no one will look for me."

"You'll be dead before you get to him," Rika said, opening her eye and leaned forward in her chair. "As much as I want him dead for what he did to my brother, I also know he won't go quietly."

"No, he won't," I said. "But if I die, at least I died doing something and not cowering or just letting him get away with it."

"He stays in his Spire," Rika said. "You got any idea how you're going to get in?"

I shook my head.

"That's not exactly optimistic," Rika said.

"I considered some climbing gear and a ghillie cloak, but that's the kind of climb that I'm not sure I could do even with the gear. Especially in the winter. The wind alone would tear me off that Spire."

"How about the mountain?" Rika asked. "You climb that, take a glider with you, you could jump down onto the roof of the Spire."

"I'm not a mountain climber," I told her. "It's one thing to ascend a smooth structure, but those mountains are going to kill anyone who isn't used to climbing them."

"The other way is a wire cannon," Rika said, although I wasn't sure if she was telling me or talking to herself.

"What's a wire cannon?"

"Ah, it's something one of my people tinkered around with. We found an old grapnel launcher, and we made some modifications."

"You *found* it?" I asked with a raised eyebrow.

"We modified it," Rika said, continuing as if I hadn't said anything. "It's less of a weapon and more of a means of escape from somewhere high. But the cable is strong enough to hold four, and there's a quick movement system we installed that will take you along the cable faster than having to crawl hand-over-hand."

"You want me to climb a separate Spire and crawl across to Trias' one. That's several hundred feet of climbing a half a mile in the air."

"We'll give you a ghillie cloak," Rika said. "We have some spare. Some kind of thermal protection too, that high up will freeze you quickly. There's only one problem though."

"Apart from being half a mile in the air, dangling from a wire while I freeze to death?"

"Yes, apart from that," Rika said, ignoring my sarcasm.

"And that is?"

"Well, technically it's two problems," Rika amended. "First of all, we haven't exactly tested it in winter. And by exactly, I mean not at all. It might go horribly wrong, but what's life if not a little risk?" She gave me a thumbs up and smiled.

"Superb," I said, rolling my eyes. "And the second thing?"

"It's going to take us twelve hours to make sure it's ready. It's currently in," she counted on her fingers. "Many pieces."

I sighed. "That actually works out," I said. "I need to get to an off-world comm relay."

Rika's laugh was loud and mocking. "And I need to be a queen," she said, clapping her hands twice and raising them above her head as if some imaginary force might see her gesture and think *sure, why not?* "Yep, that didn't work."

"Do you know where one is or not?"

"A working off-world comm?" Rika said, exhaling as she thought. "I do but you're not going to like it."

"I haven't liked anything that's happened in the last few days, why start now?"

"Good point," Rika said with an apathetic shrug. "It's at an abandoned fuel depository close to the mountains."

It took me several seconds to recall the place she was talking about. "Wait, that place was shut down because of a leak. It killed two dozen people."

Rika shrugged again. "And once everyone was gone, some enterprising souls set up an off-world comm there. Best place for it. It's empty, it's large, and no one ever goes there. Not even Blackcoats."

"How do you know about it?"

"The vendors share intel," she said as if that explained everything. "It's outside of Trias' influence, I know that much. But it's also never been used to make an actual off-world comm."

"Never used?" I repeated as it dawned on me. "Because if it was, the people in charge of this planet would immediately know about it?"

"It's been used to talk to people in other parts of the planet, but not off-world," Rika said. "So, we know it works, but the second you send a comm, you're going to light up like a beacon. It's in one of the two towers at the far end of the building. Why do you even want to use one?"

"I get a message to The Wardens, I can get Trias investigated," I explained, expecting Rika to laugh at me.

Instead, she just nodded. "Makes sense. They have no influence here at the moment. Trias is a new Councillor, and he doesn't make waves with the Council or the Union, so they have no reason to constantly hover around him. Give them a reason, and they'll swarm here. I don't think Trias would enjoy that."

"That's the plan, but I have to get the message off-world. While Blackcoats are hunting me."

"That's a you-problem," Rika said without any hostility. I knew it would be too much to expect her to help actually go against the Blackcoats. She still had her own people to consider.

"I know," I told her. "But I want you to get a message to Ekhar."

"I thought this wasn't about vengeance," Rika said mockingly.

"Of course it's about vengeance," I said, the words almost lashing out. "They killed my friend. They tried to kill me. They ruined my entire life. Vengeance is all I have left."

"At least you're honest about it,' Rika said. "I expected some self-righteous bullshit. Nice to know Blackcoats have actual feelings."

"We're not robots," I said, feeling a similar argument brewing.

"No," Rika said sadly. "Did my brother die quickly?"

"I don't know," I admitted. "I hope so."

Rika was silent for several seconds before speaking. "Why not kill you too?"

"Trias wanted to know what I know."

"And what is that, exactly? What finally tipped him over the edge to this scorched-earth policy he's undertaken?"

"He's newly elected to the Council," I said. "Doesn't want anyone to be able to link him to the crimes he's committed."

"He would certainly be concerned about The Wardens turning up and ruining his day," Rika said. "So, what did you find out?

What *exactly*?"

I wasn't sure I wanted to go into it with Rika, I wasn't sure the knowledge would cause her more problems if Trias and his people discovered it. "Energy Mist," I said. "It's a military compound. Trias was using the people of this city as his own personal lab rats and sending the data back to a Union military covert science branch."

"He was doing *what*?" Rika almost shouted. "Are you serious?"

I nodded. "Your brother and I were working on a case about someone who was selling Energy Mist that was at a much higher potency than usual. We found out that the person who was selling it had stolen it from a shipment and was selling it uncut. Trias found out, killed a lot of people to keep it from getting out, but they didn't do a good enough job. We linked the shipment we found back to the science team who created it."

"And where is that team?"

"We don't know," I admitted. "We knew they were off-world, we knew they never stayed in the same place for too long. We thought they might have had some kind of orbital station. We hoped that with Trias being investigated we could figure out who he was working with. We told our captain, and two days later he ended up dead. The next day, I got attacked in my home and..." I waved my arms around. "Here we are."

"So, you were sold out," Rika said, crossing her arms. "You think your captain did it?"

I shrugged. "No clue. I figured he was safe to talk to. Actually, I figured he was the only safe person to talk to. Your brother thought the same. If the captain spoke to someone about it, it cost him his life. And if he didn't... well, someone else sold us out. Ekhar probably."

"Ah, yes, and we come back to her," Rika said. "What did you want me to tell her?"

"Where I am," I said. "I want her to come to the comm outpost."

"To kill her or get information?"

"Both," I said.

Rika laughed. "If she helped kill my brother, I'll be happy to get her to you. I'll have to make it look real though, otherwise she'll suspect I'm helping you."

"I'm sure you'll figure it out," I said.

"There's a lot that could go wrong here," Rika said, getting to her feet. "Ekhar could figure out I'm setting her up, Trias could link you back to me. You could be getting tracked right now, although that's less of an issue considering the amount of shielding I have in this place."

"No badge," I said. "No tracker."

"Could be one inside you," Rika suggested.

"Be a weird thing to do though," I countered. "Kidnap me, threaten to kill me, but stick a tracker in me on the off chance I escape and kill a bunch of their own people doing so."

"That judge helped you escape," Rika said, unwilling to drop the subject. "He could be part of an elaborate scheme to…"

"You don't know how to finish that, do you?" I asked with a smile.

"Not really," Rika said. "I'll admit it's unlikely. It would be a somewhat pointless thing to do considering. The storm screws around with any signals on the best of days, which leads me to wonder how you're going to make sure this signal you want to send, actually gets off-world. You think The Wardens will pick up before Trias realises you're sending the message?"

I shrugged. "Guess we'll find out."

"Okay, Celine," Rika said with a loud exhale. "Twelve hours to get this sorted. I assume you don't have a data pad or something similar to take with you. That mask of yours have a heads-up display?"

"No," I said. "No HUD."

"Right, we'll get you some actually useful gear," Rika said. "Proper weapons too. At least until you return."

"And how much is this all going to cost me?" I asked, fully aware that Rika wasn't the kind of person to do things for favours.

"Trias killed my brother," Rika said, her tone hard. "Once

you're done with your comms, you get back here and we'll sort out ending Trias. If you manage to survive that, and that's a big *if*, and you can get back here, we'll take you out of the city. Or offworld, or down a mine shaft. Don't know where, but wherever it is, I never see you again."

I nodded. It was more than fair.

"You used that energy pistol?" Rika asked as I followed her through the maze of corridors that made up her place of business. A place of business that hadn't been raided by the authorities because she paid the right people. I wondered where the line was. What was Rika doing that was different to Trias? Well, Rika didn't murder my friends for one, she didn't torture innocent people, she didn't instil fear in those who had to live under her eye. Yes, they were both criminals, and yes, I probably should have treated them as such, but I'd grown up with Rika, and I trusted her. Besides, she fed me and her brother intel on criminal gangs in the district that took a lot of bad people out of the factories and away from causing harm.

"Only once, why?" I asked.

"It's old, looks like it was cobbled together from parts of other pistols."

I looked over the energy pistol that had been in my holster, and Rika was right, there was a lot of scratches and scarring of the metal. "Cheap but effective."

"Until it blows up in your hand," Rika said, taking me into a large armoury where hundreds of guns sat on racks along all four of the twenty-foot-long walls. The guns were interspersed with knives and other weapons, along with pieces of armour, some of which looked like high-grade military stuff. A large table sat in the middle of the room with more pieces of armour, along with two energy pistols that looked fresh out of the box, and a small datapad designed to sit on the wrist.

"This all for me?" I asked, unable to keep the excitement out of my voice.

"Happy birthday," Rika said with a smile as she started pointing to various pieces on the table. "Two energy pistols."

I picked up the black and grey weapons, they smelled new. They were lightweight and were almost certainly military spec. Strength settings on the side, a pressure trigger, and an overload function. The latter of which was dangerous in itself. The pistols held forty-two rounds before needing to have its coil vented to cool down, but overload fired all rounds left in one shot. I'd once seen it melt through the side of a tank. The downside was, you didn't just need to vent the coil, which normally took seconds, you had to replace the entire coil. Which took several minutes.

"I assume you want to keep the carbonate dagger?" Rika asked.

I nodded. "Probably wise." I picked up the helmet of a set of midnight blue and black ion armour. Lightweight, designed to stop a projectile, but basically completely useless against bladed weapons. They were standard issue for Union military branches.

"There's a thermal coupling inside the armour," Rika said. "Should stop you from freezing to death. The ghillie cloak will fit over the top without it being bulky. No point in giving you the cloak yet, it only has a few hours charge in it, and I figured you'd want one that'll last you the entire journey later."

"Good thinking."

"We'll make sure to get you a few other bits for when you return," Rika said. "Anything in particular?"

"Fusion rifle?"

"If we had a fusion rifle, you wouldn't need to crawl between Spires, you could just sit in one and shoot at the other. So, no, we don't have a fusion rifle."

"Blast-gun?"

"That we can do," Rika said. "We'll get one prepared for you."

Blast-guns fired hundreds of tiny, super-heated energy projectiles at once. They shredded everything they touched. You only needed to aim in the general direction of whatever it was you were angry with, to remove it from existence.

"That the grapnel launcher?" I asked, pointing to the massive contraption in the corner of the room that was spread out over a large part of the white and grey tiled floor.

"Yep," Rika said.

"It's massive," I told her, trying to figure out how I was ever going to be able to even pick it up.

"It takes three people to lift," Rika said.

"How am I getting this to the top of a Spire?"

"We'll figure that bit out when we've got it working," Rika said. "One thing at a time. Get changed, and we'll get you on your way. Twelve hours, Celine. If you're not back here by then, I'm going to assume you didn't make it and I'm going to forget you were ever here. I want vengeance for my brother, but I don't want to be the next person on Trias' hit-list."

"You won't be," I told her and got ready in my fresh gear as she stepped out of the room. I took the energy pistols apart, and put them back together again before holstering them, testing them on a quick draw. They were smoother than the last pistol, and the holsters felt better to wear.

I donned the helmet and tapped the part by my left cheek, bringing up the HUD inside the clear visor. It showed a grid of the city with my destination already mapped.

I left the armoury and caught the coil repeater rifle that Rika tossed my way. "Take this too," she said.

A quick check of the coil for wear showed it was brand new. I wasn't exactly surprised. The repeater would need to be re-levered after each shot to vent the coil, a bit like weapons I'd seen in museums that were used by people thousands of years ago on planets I'd never even been to, but it was a powerful and accurate weapon. I slung it over my back, letting the repeater nestle between my shoulder blades. I strapped the fist-sized medical bag around my thigh. You never knew when it might come in handy.

"You ready?" Rika asked.

I nodded. "Give me an hour before you call Ekhar."

"You'd better start running then," Rika said, hitting a yellow button on the wall beside her.

The gate on the opposite side of the room began to slowly rise, the cold wind whipping under the gap.

"Thank you for this," I told Rika, tapping the side of the

scarf around my throat, which automatically moved up across the lower portion of my face, hardening as it covered my mouth and nose. The black and red mask would let me breath without problems, but it also kept the cold out, and anything else unsavoury that might be floating in the air.

"Don't die," Rika said.

It was the last thing I heard before I set off to show those who had betrayed me and killed my friend, that they should have done a better job at making me dead.

CHAPTER FIVE

It turned out that having a map display my location and destination made life a whole lot less complicated while trying to navigate the increasingly horrible weather. The farther north I went, the more inhabited the district became, and I was soon running down the spider-web of alleyways that separated the two-hundred-storey megatowers that housed the vast majority of people in Euria.

On the occasion where I needed to venture out onto the main roads, I kept low and close to anything that would give me cover. More than once, I saw flashing blue and red lights in the haze, heard the low rumble of the powerful engines of a truck. The latter might not have been part of law enforcement, but I couldn't take the risk.

All the ducking and remaining alert took a toll on the amount of time I had to spend out in the elements, and by the time I spied the depository in the distance—or at least the blurred darkness in the shape of the depository—I'd been out for several hours. Rika meant it when she told me to be back in twelve hours.

The fencing around the depository was old and hadn't been maintained for several years. There were no heaters around the perimeter of the building, and while I didn't want to walk around the entire place—it was gigantic and would take an hour in itself—I was happy that I wasn't about to get jumped by a gang.

When I grabbed the wire fencing it came apart in my hand. The heating elements hadn't been maintained. The depository had been discarded, forgotten. I really hoped no new residents had taken up shelter within.

Once inside the perimeter, I spotted two large funnel-shaped heaters in the ground, each one the size of a large truck. They were designed to maintain a constant level of heat for the parking area outside of the depository. I'd been to the building once when it was up and running and it had been an impressive structure. It was a squat building, lower than any of the factories, but long, and it went deep underground. There were two towers at the far end of the complex, both of which were several hundred meters tall. If Rika was correct, and I had no reason to think she wasn't, that's where the comm relay was.

The front door and large windows on either side of the complex entrance sat in ruins, the steel bent, the glass shattered. Scorch marks touched the sides of the doorway. There had been an explosion here, presumably by the people who had wanted entry. The glass was designed to withstand a grenade, whoever had finally broken through had *really* wanted inside.

Banks of snow had built up inside the foyer beyond, and after a short and less than ideal climb up and slide down the other side, I found myself next to a large reception desk. The banks of monitors behind the desk were all destroyed.

I exited the foyer through the door to the side of the reception desk and walked along the glass-covered hallway beyond. The travelator-style floor was broken, and every footstep echoed around me, but the I was grateful to be out of the cold for now. I pulled down my face covering and pushed up my visor, keeping one hand on my pistol as I reached the only door in the hallway, and pushed it slowly open.

The room was cavernous with a variety of vehicles on plinths along one side, and several terminal monitors on the other. None of the terminals close to me appeared to be working, although several of the law enforcement vehicles that were apparently *proudly fuelled* by the depository had been graffitied to within an inch of their lives. There was a Blackcoat truck that was spray painted so much that I couldn't have even said what the original colour was. The lights on the top had been smashed too. Someone did not like

Blackcoats. I paused in front of the truck; actually pretty much no one liked Blackcoats, that was sort of the point.

Before I left the room, I spotted a working terminal flickering in the corner. I ran over and swiped on the screen, which brought up a muted info-vid about how amazing this depository was and why working here was the best thing ever, and everyone should do it. I couldn't hear the actual words, but I got the general idea, and fought down the urge to shoot the animated anthropomorphic rabbit who was telling the world how awesome everything was. Presumably.

Once the info-vid had finished, I flicked through the screens until I found a map of the facility. I scanned my own data pad device over it, and the map appeared in miniature on my wrist device.

I studied the main screen, just to be sure where I was going then set off at a heightened pace along more hallways and through rooms with increasing amounts of self-aggrandising nonsense. I ignored the majority of it; I had a reason to be here that wasn't to get irritated by a talking rabbit... right up until Trias appeared on one of the vid-screens adorning a large wall. The screen was the same size as the truck in the earlier hall, and hung from the wall, presumably so Trias' smug face could look down on everyone.

"People of Euria," he said the second I stepped within distance of the motion detection that started the vid. He raised his arms in a gesture of unity, showing off the gaudy gold and red force shield bracelet on his wrist.

Trias had pale skin and long blonde hair. He was clean shaven and had several tattoos on his arms, most of which signified him as a Councillor and priest. He wore a dark suit and white shirt, and sat on a comfortable-looking grey couch, one leg resting on the knee of the other. He smiled and showed himself to be at ease.

I wasn't entirely sure what he was saying as a white noise of rage filled my ears and I shot him in the forehead. The picture vanished and I stood in the room, looking up at the sparks coming out of the vid-screen feeling foolish for letting my anger get the better of me. Still, I had to admit I felt better for killing the bastard, even if it was only in vid-form.

Whatever locks had once been in place to stop people from getting through doors with big signs on the front saying *staff only*, were all broken. I followed the directions on my data pad through one such set of doors and found myself away from the glossy face of the depository. There were no smiling faces on big screens, only metal walkways and ladders to take you deeper into the bowels of the building.

The door at the end of the walkway took me to another identical walkway and I began to see how easy it would be to get lost in this place. I continued on for some time, going down (or up) the occasional ladder, as the smell of oil and the hiss of steam from one of the automated vents far below me became stronger. I wondered about them, wondered why the vents outside were left to rot, and the interior of the building allowed to fall into ruin, but the automated vents deep inside the structure were still working. Maybe they were just better made, or maybe the people who had set up the comm had decided to make sure the interior of the building didn't freeze. I pushed the thought aside and continued on.

Eventually, the little map on my screen took me through a set of thick metal doors that squealed in protest when I pushed them open. Once through, I found myself in a large cylindrical room with a set of stairs to the left of me that vanished behind the wall of the cylinder. Up above snow swirled, thick glass protecting me from the elements. There had to be a room at the top of that staircase, although I couldn't see it from where I stood. I sighed; that was my destination, and that was where the comm relay was going to be. I hoped.

There was nothing except old oil stains and rust in the room I now stood in, so I moved on. Elevator doors stood just next to the staircase, but it was out of order because of course it was, so I started on my climb just to add fuel to the fire that was my life.

My legs ached by the time I reached the summit. I looked over the ledge at the ground far below me. It was maybe fifty or sixty meters in all, and I didn't look forward to the climb back down.

Apart from the view, the small landing held only a painted blue metal door which was slightly ajar. Whoever was inside the room beyond wasn't even trying to keep quiet.

"Took your time," Ekhar said as I pushed open the door, revealing a spacious room with several banks of monitors, none of which were on. A large screen sat on one wall, and was attached to a ramshackle device about the same size as me.

"That's the comm relay," Ekhar said, following my gaze as I tried with all my might not to kill her where she sat.

"You betrayed me," I said, looking back at the woman who used to be my friend.

"I did."

"At least you're honest about it," I said with a slight shake of my head as an unwanted chuckle escaped my mouth.

"I assume you made sure I'd come here because you want answers," Ekhar asked. "How'd you know I wouldn't bring back-up?"

"I didn't," I said with a shrug. "I figured I'd just kill them too."

Ekhar's mouth dropped open in surprise for a moment, but quickly closed again. "You're not just some Blackcoat with previous Union military training like the rest of us. Trias got your file unlocked after your escape. Or tried to. You did some shady shit I imagine. What were you? Honour Guard? Special Operations?"

"Orbital Shock Trooper," I said, seeing no reason to lie. It wasn't like Ekhar was going to be in a position to tell anyone after.

"You were in the OST?" Ekhar asked, her expression looking like she'd just found out the worst possible news at the worst possible time.

I nodded.

"So, Trias has an ex-OST after him?" Ekhar started to laugh. "He has no idea, he thinks you're ex-special ops or something."

"Technically the OST are special-ops."

"Yes, the special-ops of special-ops," Ekhar said. "So, I came here to die."

I nodded again.

"You want to know why I did it first?"

I shrugged again. "Money, power, or a combination of the

two."

"The money was good," Ekhar said. "Do you know that I was put in your district to keep an eye on you? I wasn't meant to actually become friends with you, but I liked you. Couldn't help it. Liked Prasan too. He was a good guy. I didn't kill him, by the way, that was Trias himself. Wanted to make the Blackcoats watch while he murdered one of our own.

"When I was told that I would be going after you myself, I refused. I didn't want to be the one to get you. I understood you were now a liability to Trias, that he could no longer ignore your need to *do the right thing* or whatever bullshit code you live by. But I didn't want to be the one to do it. Right until Trias told me either I kill you, or he would kill Jaxson. Not much of a choice at all after that."

"Does your husband know you work for Trias?" I asked, not wanting to break the flow of the confession, but still wanting to check.

Ekhar nodded. "Jaxson liked you. I told him what I'd been ordered to do, and he told me that we could run. We couldn't run. He suggested using an off-world comm relay to contact The Wardens, but the second someone did that, your life would be forfeit. Your life already is, so I guess it doesn't matter to you. He's in their *care* now because you escaped your confines."

"They kidnapped him because I escaped?" I asked, feeling sick.

Ekhar nodded again. "The guards who were with me when we took you were all killed, but Trias doesn't like failure. He doesn't like to waste potential though, so killing a Blackcoat who works for him isn't so easy. He had Jaxson kidnapped from our own home. They killed our neighbours too. Family of three. For the crime of living next to me."

"You can help me," I suggested knowing she'd never go for it.

"Nope," Ekhar said. "I was there when Prasan died. I saw what they did to him. I've been told that I either bring you in dead or alive, or that's my fate. I won't be strung up like that. I can't let my husband be strung up like that. So I have to kill you."

"I can't let that happen."

Ekhar got to her feet, raising her arms to show she had no weapons on her. None that I could see, anyway. "I thought about just killing you, just doing it and getting it over with," Ekhar said. "But I really did like you. Do like you. I think you deserve a chance."

"You want to fight me unarmed?" I asked, unable to keep the shock from my voice.

Ekhar nodded. "Or I did, before I realised you were OST, now it feels stupid. But I've made my decision. I'll let you die with honour."

I blinked as if I'd misheard her. "You showed me no honour when you took me from my home. You showed me no honour when you handed me over to Trias and stood by and watched him murder one of us. Why start now?"

Ekhar's smile turned into a large grin as she lifted her leg and removed a carbonate-fibre dagger from inside her boot.

"You're going to die, Ekhar," I said. "Trias too, along with anyone else who tries to stop me."

"If you win, I hope you manage it," she said. "Please try to get Jaxson out of the Spire. That's where they take all their... projects. No way to escape the Spire, too many guards, too many floors."

"I'll do my best," I told her, and meant it. Jaxson didn't deserve to die because his wife was working for a psychopath.

"You want to do this here?" Ekhar asked.

"I don't much care," I said, my hand on my pistol. I wanted to shoot her, I wanted to get it done, but I knew if I just did that, I would regret it. She had been my friend, and while she had betrayed me, I could at least give her the chance to beat me one-on-one, which with my previous training wasn't much of a chance at all, but it was better than just being shot in the head.

I removed my holster with the pistols inside, my helmet, and scoped coil repeater rifle, placing them all in a neat pile next to the comm-relay, while keeping Ekhar in my field of vision. She'd been my friend, but she'd been working for the enemy and had betrayed me. Besides just because someone had once been my friend, didn't mean I was suddenly an idiot.

I drew the carbonate-fibre dagger from the sheath on my hip. I didn't want to have a knife fight. Knife fights are unpleasant. No one ever comes out of a knife fight without getting hurt, and then even if you win, you still lose. The OST were taught to use bladed weapons to kill during drops into hostile territory, but that's a different set of circumstances to actually fighting someone else also wielding a knife.

"When you're dead, this will all be over," Ekhar said, sounding as if she didn't quite believe it.

I took a deep breath and stepped toward her, exhaling slowly as I moved.

Ekhar wasted no time and darted toward me, her dagger flashing up toward my chest, trying to catch me unaware.

I stepped aside, pushed her arm away and smashed my elbow across her face with a crack that knocked her to the side. She staggered away and waved the knife back at me in an attempt to stop a follow-up attack, but I was already moving back, putting distance between us.

When Ekhar looked back up at me, the lower half of her face was bloody. I'd broken her nose. Good.

Ekhar spat blood onto the metal floor and sprang at me, moving her knife around to try and catch me off guard. I slashed up, across the back of her hand, and she dropped the knife, catching it with the other, and flicked it across my ribs. The armour that was designed to stop a projectile held fast from the blade, but as I moved back, she brought the knife up, cutting me along the back of my forearm and smiling as I pushed her away.

I brought my own knife down in an arc, aiming for her face, but she deflected the knife with her own and punched me in the face as my attention was on making sure she didn't stab me.

I was cut, bruised, and felt more than a little stupid for leaving myself open. I *really* hate knife fights.

Ekhar stepped toward me, her knife flashing up toward my face, I cut her hand again, and when she stepped away I followed her, nicking her cheek and slicing through her earlobe before she could put distance between us.

The armour Ekhar wore protected her torso, so making a killing stab to it would have been difficult, although not impossible with enough force. Death by a thousand cuts was always possible, and there were enough exposed or low-armoured parts of her body to make that a reality.

Ekhar reached into the pocket of her trousers.

"I assume fighting fair is over," I said.

She rushed me once more, and I deflected her blade with my knife, before turning it and bringing it up under her guard, just below her ribs. She gasped in pain as the force of the blow cut through her armour and sank into flesh. I twisted the knife, and she grabbed my hand, scratching it.

My world spun, and I took a step back, my now-bloody knife still in my hand.

"What did you do?" I demanded.

"I was going to do this with honour," Ekhar said, showing me the metal claw tips on two of her fingers that glistened with my blood and something much worse. "But honestly, honour is going to get me killed."

She brought the knife down toward me, but I launched myself up at her, pushing her arm away and headbutting her in the face with everything I had. Ekhar screamed in pain as I followed up with a second headbutt, and a third, before smashing my elbow into her broken nose and kicking her in the chest hard enough to throw her back.

She took one look at me, bloody and presumably drugged, and turned tail, running out of the room.

I raced to the exit as the sounds of voices came up from below.

"She's up there," Ekhar shouted at allies I couldn't see. "Kill her already."

I half ran, half swayed back to my gear and hurriedly put it on, drawing the coil rifle. The time for honour was over. Now was the time to kill every godsdamned one of them.

CHAPTER SIX

I had no idea what I'd been drugged with, but it wasn't getting any worse than slight dizziness and an overwhelming need to lay down and go to sleep. I removed a small adrenaline shot from the medical bag still against my leg, and after removing the cap, plunged the inch-long needle just above the strap on my thigh. The effect was immediate: I threw up.

My first thought after it happened was that I hoped no one saw me, and the second was that I hoped it had gotten rid of whatever shit Ekhar had used on me. Thankfully, I felt much less dizzy and the nausea was quickly gone, replaced with an overwhelming desire to hurt a lot of people in my way of finishing the job with Ekhar. I'd given her the honour she'd asked for, and she'd thrown it back in my face by using a poison on me. No more games, no more niceties, no more honour. Just blood and death.

"She's in the room at the top of the tower," a man's voice shouted as I heard steps thundering up the long staircase toward me. I had time.

I sheathed my carbonate-fibre blade and moved back into the room, activating the comm-tower. It gave off a low buzzing noise as a power-level indicator on the front panel showed zero percent. *Superb.*

I ran back to the exit and aimed the rifle down the stairs. It would take the soldiers a while to get to me if my own journey up the stairs was any indication, and they were also bottlenecked. Not exactly the smartest decision on their part to come for me here.

The elevator pinged.

I moved quickly, raising my rifle as the doors opened revealing an empty elevator. I swung the rifle back to the only other exit as the elevator exploded.

I was ten feet away when it happened, and it wasn't enough explosives to destroy the room or tower itself, but the blast was focused out directly in front of the open doors, just enough to kill anyone who had gone over to find out why an empty elevator had just arrived.

I was thrown back, over a set of monitors and hit the floor hard, knocking the air from my lungs as the first of the armed guards entered the room. I spotted them as I lay on the floor, and rolled under the desk, hidden from view for the moment while I caught my breath. The repeater was still in my hand, and my ears still rang from the explosion, the armour having saved my life: although it was more than a little singed.

It took me a few seconds to control my breathing, roll out from under the desk and come up onto my feet, firing into the head of the closest guard, before hitting the next two in succession as they turned away from the elevator. A fourth guard entered the room and took a repeater shot to the forehead, his helmet offering no protecting from the power of the round.

I moved the rifle to find anyone else, but was barrelled into from behind, taking me off my feet, and forcing me to drop the weapon. My attacker threw me over the banks of monitors where I landed hard on the floor, rolling to the side as a guard vaulted over, driving his foot down onto where my head had been seconds before.

I got to my feet in time to block a kick to the chest from the guard and managed to put a little distance between us. My ears still rang, and my head was beginning to swim again, either from the explosion or from the effects of the poison that was still in my system. The adrenaline shot wouldn't last forever, and I didn't even know how many guards had come to kill me.

The entrance to the room was in front of me, with the guard between me and it. The comm unit was behind me, hopefully undamaged, although I hadn't the time to check. It beeped occasionally, a beautiful sound as the ringing in my ears stopped and I discovered I didn't have serious damage to them.

The guard had a shock baton in one hand. No gun. Weird. The explosion wasn't meant to kill me, just knock me silly so they could come in and finish up.

"You took me alive once before," I said, rolling my shoulders. "Didn't work out so well for you."

"Trias wants to hear you scream before you die," the guard said.

"You first," I told him and drew my pistol shooting him in the head, which rocked back but did little else. The helmet he was wearing had saved his life, and the energy pistol spluttered once before dying, a piece of shrapnel in the barrel.

The man removed his helmet, rolled his own shoulders, and I shot him in the head with the second pistol. That one worked.

I checked the pistol as two small metal spheres bounced into the room: cluster grenade. The guards had decided me being dead was preferable to them being dead.

I threw myself over the bank of monitors and rolled under them as the grenades exploded, shredding everything within ten feet with thousands of tiny particles that were perfectly harmless right up until the casing cracked open and exposed them to air. I'd seen cluster grenades tear into battle armour like it was made of paper. Fortunately for me, cluster grenades have a very small kill-zone radius. While anything within six feet was going to be torn to pieces, anything beyond that was mostly going to find themselves with some nasty bruising and an unpleasant headache.

Pieces of the roof began to fall directly above where the grenades had exploded, and from the crack in the desk, I spotted the plaster around the entrance had been removed entirely, exposing the steel-skeleton of the tower inside.

I rolled back out from under the desk and hurried over to the entrance as the first guard came in, the barrel of his blast-gun rifle protruding into the room before he did. Grabbing it with one hand, I yanked it up and shot him in the chest with my energy pistol. It took four rapid shots in the exact same place, but it eventually punched a hole through the armour and into his chest, killing him.

I kicked his lifeless body back down the stairs, taking out the legs of two guards as they tried in vain to avoid him. I fired the energy pistol at the two guards, catching one of them in the neck, which sprayed the other in blood as his artery was obliterated.

The other guard was dead a moment later when I slammed my dagger up under his chin. I kicked his body down the steps and drew my pistol, walking down the staircase with knife and pistol in hand, ready for whatever was next.

I reached the halfway point when I realised that everyone else in the tower was dead. That didn't mean it was the end of my trouble, but it did mean a brief respite from having to kill all of Trias' men. I retraced my steps, the dizziness settling in as I reached the room. I had to lean up against the remains of the doorway and take a moment to catch my breath. My body was screaming at me to find somewhere to hide and ride out whatever Ekhar had dumped into my body, but I didn't have time to do that. I needed to finish the mission.

The mission. I sighed. How easily old habits return.

The comm relay was a little dirty, and had some blood splatter, but thankfully nothing to stop it charging. I found my coil repeater and sat down beside the relay while the panel read ninety percent. My pistol and knife were placed back in their respective holsters, and I kept the repeater aimed at the door. The rifle was proven to punch through the guard's armour, it was why they were illegal to own in Euria.

The incessant beeping of the comm-relay a few moments later made me jump as I'd been so focused on the doorway. I got to my feet and tapped the panel, bringing up a new screen to put coordinates. I knew them off by heart, The Wardens headquarters on the planet of Atharoth, several systems away. The seat of power in Union space.

"This is Blackcoat Celine Moro," I said into the relay. "I'm on the planet Xolea, the city of Euria. Our Councillor is Trias Nateria.

He is a corrupt individual who has used his own power to murder and subjugate his own people. I have evidence of his crimes, but his people are hunting me. I have evidence of his working with a black ops science project to force a drug onto the people of this city. A drug that turns people into monsters with enough exposure. I need your help."

I paused.

"Please," I continued. "I can't do this alone. I can't stop more people from dying horrific deaths alone. He's killing Blackcoats, he has even more in his pocket. He's a monster. Please send The Wardens to the coordinates with this message. Please help us."

I sent the message, and put it on a repeating loop of every ten minutes until it was switched off. I just hoped that someone would get it and do something about what was happening.

I dropped to my knees and wept, my emotions and exhaustion getting the better of me. The room was swimming now, but the job wasn't done. I had to get back to Rika. I forced myself to stand; leant against the comm relay to make sure I wasn't about to fall over, and when steady, walked toward the exit of the room. And promptly fell over.

Beside me was the body of one of the guards I'd killed. The lucky bastard.

I got back to my feet, and when that didn't work out, leaned against the wall and slowly slid down to a seated position. The adrenaline had worn off, and I felt sleepy. I was pretty sure that whatever was coursing through my system wasn't designed to kill me. I felt more high than being near death, but either way, it wasn't a pleasant feeling and I wanted it to be over with.

I rummaged in the medical pouch and came up with nothing that might help me, although there was some pain medication and a food supplement bar that looked like it had been run over by a truck. Great. I forced myself to my feet and made my way over to the elevator, using it to go back down as I figured using the stairs was a recipe for a painful disaster.

The facility felt eerier now with all the dead bodies in it, especially considering I'd put most of them there, and I expected to have to deal with Ekhar and her companions every time I entered a new room. Thankfully, my paranoia was unfounded, but it didn't shake the feeling that we weren't done. Ekhar wouldn't have brought a dozen guards with her and then just leave. She'd have gotten back-up.

I reached the museum room where I'd shot the vid of Trias and paused. Something felt wrong, and not just the fact that whatever Ekhar had done to me was making me *really* hungry. My stomach growled.

"Down, girl," I said, pointing to my stomach. I giggled and immediately clamped my hands over my mouth. *What the hell was that?*

I ate the food supplement bar, wondering if the truck that had run over it had improved the taste of it in any way. When done, my head felt a little less foggy and I no longer wanted to go to sleep. I needed to find more food though, I was still hungry.

Unfortunately, I knew that Ekhar might be waiting for me outside. It had been a thought that I'd considered the entire way through the facility, but after the head fog had started to clear, it was the one remaining consideration.

I brought up the map of the facility on my data pad, and had it project the map above my wrist. I used my other hand to move the map around, zooming in and out until I found what I was looking for: a second way out.

Actually, there were eight ways out of the building, but only one of them took me down to the tunnel under the facility. A tunnel from which I could vanish into the network under the city. Ekhar would have people down there, but the tunnels came in two types: the large one used for the trams and shipping, and the small one or two person tunnels used for maintenance staff. Any guards down there were going to have a hard time of getting out.

Before I decided to take a detour though, I exited through the door at the end of the museum and took the staircase to the floor above. An automat machine sat at the top of the stairs, in the middle of a large open-planned area surrounded by dozens of offices. All of the offices had glass walls, and while some thought it looked nice and relaxed, I always thought it was so management could watch everyone easier. Several of the offices had eerie lights flickering inside.

I broke the glass of the automat and removed several more of the same food supplement bars. They were in date for decades, so I wasn't worried about spoiled food. I ate two as I made my way along the hall to the giant glass windows at the end that overlooked the front of the building.

There was a behemoth on the forecourt of the building. And three dozen heavily armed guards. The behemoth was overkill. It was twenty-feet tall, sat on two huge legs, and was heavily armoured. A plasma chain-canon attached to one arm, a missile battery to the other, and a massive sword that was thankfully still sheathed against its back. They were used a lot in the war. There were one, two, and three pilot versions, each with a different function. The one stood in the forecourt had its pilot cockpit open, the pilot stood beside the imposing monster, talking to... Ekhar.

All that firepower for me. It really was overkill. *Trias must be worried*. Lower maintenance access was the way to go. I did not want to have to fight a behemoth with two energy pistols, a carbonate-fibre dagger, a coil repeater rifle, and my sour attitude.

I double-timed it as quickly as I dared back down the stairs, and followed them down two floors until I was under the building. After eating another of the supplement bars I'd stolen from the automat, my head wasn't swimming anymore, and I no longer felt the unnerving urge to giggle. I should kill Ekhar for that alone.

I took the stairwell as far down as I dared, ignoring the partially opened doors to dark floors I neither had the time, nor inclination, to search. Whatever secrets they might have held would just have to stay that way for someone else to find.

At the bottom floor, I found the large white door with *Staff Only* written in big blue letters across it. The door-scanner was powered down, and I flicked it with one gloved finger. My head now feeling something akin to normality. Whatever the stuff Ekhar had pumped into me, it had been short-lived, and eating had helped absorb it.

When I'd first signed on as a Blackcoat, I'd had to do rigorous training for several months, and once I'd passed, I was taken to a small room inside Blackcoat HQ and told that while flashing my badge would get me into most places, there was another way. I smashed the scanner with the butt of my repeater, brushing the fragments of smart glass aside to get to the wiring behind. With a powerful, upward tug on the wires, there was the *click* I was looking for. The panel moved slightly, revealing the mechanism behind.

This method of getting into doors was only to be used in an emergency as it completely ruined the door and made sure it was never useable again, but as all doors in factories were made by the same company, all of them had the same safety mechanism. A mechanism no one was meant to know except executives and Blackcoats. A safety mechanism kept from the people it might actually help to keep safe summed up the entire planet quite well.

Inside the panel was a blue and red striped lever, I pulled it down and there was a slight hiss and a click. The doors inched apart, and were easy to manoeuvre now. As I stepped into whatever waited for me beyond, the lights stopped flickering, illuminating a large room with several benches along one wall, and a reception desk on the other. Two doors sat in front of me—one blue, one yellow. I had no idea what either meant, but I was certain that some level of power had been maintained in the labs. I wasn't sure if that was good or bad news.

"Celine." A familiar voice sounded out all around me. "You can hear me, yes?"

Ekhar had gotten into the facility's communications. Fantastic.

"I know you're not dead, it wouldn't be that easy," Ekhar continued. "So, I wanted to let you know a little about the facility. You see, Celine, officially it was a fuel depository. But was, in reality, a front for the same scientific group who created Energy Mist."

That did not sound good. I made my way to the blue door, and behind it lay a long hallway with glass on the right. Beyond the glass was a large office, the only entrance and exit through the yellow door. Looked like I'd picked the right one.

"I wish I could see your face," Ekhar said. "How're you feeling with the drugs? Tired?"

"Will you shut up?" I shouted, fully aware Ekhar couldn't hear me, but feeling better for shouting it anyway.

On the left-hand side of the hallway were several more offices, presumably for the important people who worked here. I walked to the end where there was another blue door, and opened it, revealing a huge open room that was at least a hundred feet long and fifty feet wide. There were a dozen work stations inside the room with terminals at each one. Two doors sat at the end, another blue one, accompanied by a red one. I took the blue door and found another corridor. The map on my wrist told me it led to a staircase and several rooms that upon viewing appeared to be break rooms. The red door went… nowhere.

"I'm getting bored talking to myself," Ekhar said. "I really do hope you get to find out what they were doing in there, I wish I could see your face. You know, before it's torn off and used like a napkin."

I ignored Ekhar and tapped the map. How could the red door go to nowhere? I continued down the hallway from the blue door and found a break room and several meeting rooms. Everything was on the left-hand side of the hallway, and the righthand side was solid. What were they hiding? And why did I *really* not want to find out? I hurried my pace and pushed open the door at the end of the hallway into another large room just like the map said.

The room had one blue door, which was on the map, and one set of huge metal doors which weren't. The map said that the tunnel exit was through the blue door, along another corridor, through two more doors, and down a set of stairs. I ignored the metal doors and continued the way I was meant to go.

The hallway beyond had a glass wall like the first, there were containers hanging from the ceiling. Three dozen of them, each one with green or purple liquid inside. I stared through the glass at the containers and more than once spotted movement inside them. Nothing good was inside those containers.

There was a noise behind me, the scrapping of metal on metal.

"Come outside and I'll kill you quickly," Ekhar said. "You have thirty seconds."

I moved back toward the sound, knowing I probably shouldn't, but wanting to make sure I wasn't about to be ambushed by something. I pushed the door open, and the room beyond was identical to how it had been, except the metal double doors were now open. I did not need to know what was inside, and immediately turned and sprinted back down the corridor.

"Fifteen," Ekhar said, cheerfully.

I hit the blue door on the opposite side of the hallway. It didn't budge.

"Ten," Ekhar continued.

"Shut up," I shouted again, smashing the control panel and performing the same routine to open the door as I'd done to get into the laboratory area. That's what this place was, a lab for creating... I didn't want to know.

"One and a half," Ekhar said, and I thought I heard a laugh in her voice.

I got the door to budge and slipped inside, ending in a small room with only one blue door, which was thankfully already ajar.

"Three-quarters," Ekhar continued as I forced the doors as closed as they could be.

"Zero," Ekhar finished. "Chance over, Celine. Goodbye."

The entire facility was plunged into darkness, a second later flickering lights on the floor bathed everything in a deeply unpleasant pale glow. I placed a hand on my pistol as somewhere behind came the sound of glass breaking.

CHAPTER SEVEN

My brain screamed at me to run, but I wasn't sure if I would be running into trouble or away from it. Besides, I didn't want to give away my position to whatever had broken the glass. My heart raced, I had no idea what I was dealing with, and no idea what I was going to do about it. So, I did the only thing I could think of, and continued toward my original objective.

It was doubtful that Ekhar had placed any guards in the tunnels now, considering she'd just released something from inside the labs. She expected it—or them—to finish me off before I reached the exit.

I followed the map on my data-pad until I reached the stairwell, resisting the urge to bound down them like a child waking up on their birthday and going downstairs for presents. Although, hopefully with a lot less terror coursing through their minds.

I'd made it down three flights when scraping from high above had me still, my breathing surely giving me away considering how loud it sounded. My heart pounded. I had no idea why I was so afraid. Maybe the remnants of whatever I'd been drugged with? Maybe I was losing my edge? I shook my head; definitely not the latter.

The decision to keep moving forward was an easy one; no one wants to stay still while something unidentified decides to make you their next meal. The scraping from above was louder now and was followed by an almighty bang, and roar that shook me to my bones.

I gave up on being quiet and took the steps two at a time, bounding down the stairwell to burst through the partially open door at the bottom and taking off at a flat sprint down the tunnel beyond. My footsteps echoed around the narrow, dimly lit space, the prickles of gooseflesh on the back of my neck rising with each step, but I dared not stop or slow, and I certainly wasn't about to look behind me.

I hit the door at the opposite end at high speed, and it swung open, slamming shut behind me as I found myself in a room with several benches and two doors. One had the word *tram* written on it in big yellow letters, which gave a pretty good idea about where it went, and the other was just coloured blue. I grabbed the nearest bench and pulled it behind the door, jamming it between the sides. It wasn't going to do much to anything determined, but it should give me a few seconds. I yanked open the blue door and ran down the tunnel. It was big enough for two people side-by-side, and I had my energy pistol out just in case I'd been wrong about Ekhar, but the tunnel was empty.

The tunnel twisted and turned as it moved deeper underground. As I reached another blue door and pushed it open to leave, roars and screams of rage bounced down the tunnel toward me. What in the name of the Union had Ekhar unleashed?

I'd pushed into a large loading area where machinery used for loading and unloading had long since been left, and there were four large containers in the corner next to a huge metal shutter with the word *Tram* written on it. According to the data-pad, the exit was to the north through a maintenance door, but there was another exit to the side—a large set of double-wide shutters that led up and out to the side of the building.

I ran over to the double doors and smashed my fist against the big blue button beside them. The motors inside the wall churned and whirled for a second, and finally the shutters began to open. I sprinted over to the maintenance tunnel and practically dove inside, pulling the door shut behind me with a satisfying click.

The exhale of breath that followed was the most beautiful I'd had in recent memory. The screams and howls outside of the door were not. I backed away and set off down the maintenance tunnel. According to the data-pad, it would take me out of the facility and into a large parking area that I'd been in before—although I'd had no idea it was linked to a fuel depository. It was several miles away though, so I had a long walk ahead of me. As much as I wanted to sprint the distance, I didn't want to alert whatever unpleasant things were behind me. Besides, having a long walk was probably better than what Ekhar had planned.

According to my data-pad, I made it two hundred feet when I found that the tunnel had collapsed. "I don't know who's messing with me, but I'd really like them to stop," I muttered with an exasperated sigh.

I retraced my steps, stopping outside of the door of the maintenance tunnel and pressed my ear against the metal but heard nothing. The energy pistol had been in a firm grip for some time now, and I was grateful for its company, but right there I wished I'd had something with a lot more firepower. I sighed and slowly pushed the door open.

The sounds of things scrambling about in the loading area made me want to shut the door again, something didn't *feel* right. Being in proximity of these things made me afraid. I'd seen and fought creatures in a dozen systems that could have easily taken my head clean off, and hadn't been afraid. I'd just done the job I needed.

One of the creatures skittered past a loading machine and I paused. It was human sized, but ran on all fours, its arms elongated, like it had been partially stretched. It wore no clothing, and its skin was a mixture of red and bright pink splotches. I saw no hair on it.

I remained where I was as the creature walked, still on all fours, slowly back around the loading machine. It stopped when it saw me and stared. Its face had at one point been human, but its mouth now had a slit along either side, running from each corner of its lips, up along its cheeks, and stopping under its ears. Its nose was flat and over-wide, squashed almost, and its eyes were black pools of nothingness. What had been done to these people?

It screamed, the slits along the side of its face allowing the creatures mouth to open much wider, like a snake, revealing rows of small teeth that were designed to rend flesh from bone. Fear jolted through me, and I almost took a step back.

"You're making me afraid," I said to the creature, which stopped walking toward me and sniffed the air as I shot it in the mouth twice, blasting out the back of its head.

That made me feel better.

The high-pitched shriek the creature let out as it died made my head hurt, but before I could clamp my hands over my ears, two more of the creatures seemed to magically appear atop one of the large containers.

I shot the first one through the shoulder, knocking it face-first to the metal container with a noise like wet rags slapping the floor. The second creature launched itself from the top of the twenty-foot-high container. I dodged aside but the creature was remarkably quick and caught my arm, spinning me around and throwing me across the loading area.

I landed hard, rolled, and realised I'd narrowly missed hitting a loader headfirst. My energy pistol was still in my hand, and I shot the creature, taking a part of its jaw off with the first blast, but it was on me before I could get a second shot away.

What had once been fingers were now misshapen claws and it tried to gain purchase on my armour, attempting to rip it open. The damn thing was incredibly strong, and it pinned my arm under me as it tried to find the weakness in my armour. I twisted, fired the energy pistol up into its head, killing it then shooting the third out of the air as it leapt toward me.

I crashed back onto the ground, breathing hard as a fourth creature slowly moved out of an open container on the far side of the loading bay. It was bigger than the other three, its head encased in bone armour the colour of putrid flesh. It roared at me and charged. I shot it twice in the head, but the rounds did nothing to the charging creature.

I threw myself to the side and, rolling back to my feet, ran around one of the large loaders as the creature gave chase. I activated the overload function on my energy pistol, and climbed up onto the loader, jumping into the driver's seat and slamming the thick glass door shut. The creature slammed into the door, clawed the glass, splintering it but not punching through.

It jumped onto the flatbed at the front of the loader, pacing up and down, never taking its eyes from me. The overload charge beeped, I kicked open the glass door, and the creature roared as it ran toward me. I raised the pistol and fired.

The entire head and shoulders of the creature vanished in a plume of gore. It staggered forward, and fell to the flatbed, tumbling off the side of the loader with a sickening thud.

The energy pistol was fried. It would need its internal coil replaced and I didn't exactly have a spare on me. It was now a very expensive ornament. I put it back in its holster, just in case I found a coil I could use, and climbed down out of the loader, dropping the last few feet to the floor beside the dead... thing. They had been human. Someone needed to pay for that.

The metal shutters I'd opened were still up and I followed the mass of footprints until I could hear the chaos of snarling and gunfire. There was a battle going on up ahead, and when I reached the end of the long ramp out of the loading area and crouched behind a wall, I peered around the corner at the fighting.

There was *a lot* of fighting. The creatures numbered in their dozens, and even more were already dead. The guards had gone from a few dozen to just fifteen... thirteen as two of them were attacked by one of the big creatures I'd just killed. It ripped one guard in half and tore the head off another. If anything, it looked to be even bigger than the one I'd killed. Because even bigger monsters were exactly what right then called for.

One of the guards fired in my direction, making his choice of priority between killing me and defending himself against a horde of creatures somewhat of a strange one. He should have gone with the creatures as he was missing his head and legs a few seconds later when five of the things tore him to pieces.

Twelve.

The behemoth was motionless at the far end of the forecourt, next to the gates of the facility. That was my destination, but it took me a while to realise why it wasn't fighting. The pilot was currently in at least two pieces beside the behemoth's feet. A large creature was happily feasting on one half.

I ducked back down behind the wall and checked my resources. Despite frying one energy pistol, I still had one left, which had several shots fired from it, but it was enough. I had my coil rifle. And I had a dagger, although if it ever got to the point where I was fighting those things with a dagger, I was already dead.

The wind whipping across the forecourt mercifully meant I didn't have to hear the screams of horror as the guards were butchered. I was pretty sure Ekhar would have run for it the second she saw the creatures coming toward her. Running was apparently her best feature.

I unslung my coil repeater rifle and stepped out from behind the wall, looking down the scope, and putting the first round through the back of the head of the closest creature as it looked up from its feeding. I vented the coil and put the second round through the head of the creature that had been beside its now headless friend. Two down, more to go than I was really happy with.

I took a few steps toward the fighting, shooting at the creatures closest, trying to thin the herd as the main group were still involved in heavy fighting with the guards who hadn't fled or been eaten.

The sounds of growling from the creatures, and cries of pain from their victims cut through the wind as I neared. I'd killed six creatures from a distance, but they'd been the ones at the far rim of the carnage. Those remaining were in closer groups, and in bigger numbers. Picking off one or two wasn't going to do the trick anymore.

I stopped by a partially masticated guard who had opted to shoot himself in the head rather than the considerably worse option that was coming his way. The creature was dead beside him, I'd killed the thing myself. I removed two cluster grenades from the belt of the dead guard, hanging them from my own while keeping one eye on the fighting. The surviving guards had decided to give up on fighting me, far too preoccupied with not being the next meal for an horrific monster, but I knew the second they felt safe, that would quickly change.

A blast gun went off in my direction, but I rolled to the side and watched as the super-hot particles shredded the remains of the dead guard and monster.

"Seriously?" I shouted and fired the coil repeater in the guard's direction, taking him in the shoulder and spinning around to the ground, where several of the creatures descended before he could escape. I shot two of the monsters before the other three recognised me as a threat and turned my way. I should have left the stupid idiot guard to die but being eaten alive wasn't something I'd wish on my worst enemy. Well, maybe my *worst* enemy, but not some stupid asshole who was too dumb to recognise the true threat.

Two more coil-repeater shots in quick succession killed two more creatures, before something hit me in the back. I rolled with the blow, watching as a set of massive jaws narrowly missed where my head had been. I removed a cluster grenade and activated it, throwing it into the open maw of the advancing creature.

The creatures' jaw snapped shut around the grenade before the entire front half of the thing vanished in a roar of noise and gore. Those creatures close enough to the death of the large one that had just tried to eat me, turned toward me—a new threat more important than whatever they'd been doing. I tossed the second cluster grenade into a group of six creatures, who all watched it roll beyond them. They were already dead, limbs and flesh cartwheeling through the air as I got back to my feet and shot the closest remaining creature through the eye.

The eight living guards, having figured out that we were, for now, on the same side, attacked the creatures with a new determination to not be eaten.

When the fighting was done, and the creatures were annihilated, four guards remained. Two of them had run out of ammo for whatever weapons they carried and had settled for using knives to kill the last few creatures. One guard appeared to be bleeding out from a nasty wound on her leg.

My coil repeater was still in my hand and there were two dozen gore covered feet between me and their group.

"You want to do this?" I asked. The wind had died down now, although the snow still fell in clumps. They heard me without trouble.

The guard closest to me still had his blast gun aimed in my direction. I doubted the particles inside would do a lot of damage to me at the distance I was, and with the wind around us, and from the look on his face, he knew it. But he also didn't want to lower the gun. We were at an impasse. They couldn't go back and say I'd escaped; I couldn't let them kill me.

"Your friend needs help," I said. "I'm going to take that behemoth and leave. You can tell Trias I got inside and escaped as you were trying to kill all these things. You can tell him I died in there if you like. Tell him what you want, make it as outlandish and ludicrous as you can think, but if you want to go right now, you'll all die here and your fighting to survive will mean nothing."

"She killed a dozen of those things without blinking," one of the guards said.

"She's wounded," the guard with the gun said, his voice wavering.

I was wounded, that was true. I'd taken a nasty cut to my arm that had gone through my amour when one of the creatures had gotten a little too close to use their claws on me. I'd killed that creature with an energy pistol shot to the head, I still had one pistol left, but it was running low on ammo. I was mostly just banged up and bruised, but that just meant I was a little slower than I'd like, would feel the majority of the pain the next day. Seeing how I didn't think I was going to live that long, I guessed it didn't much matter how I currently felt.

"Go or die," I said, my words hard, my eyes narrowing. I slung my coil repeater over my shoulder and let my left-hand hover over my holstered energy pistol. Four guards, four shots. I was pretty sure I could take them all before any of them drew on me.

The blast-gun would be first to die, he was the only one with a gun out. One couldn't even hold a gun, and one looked like they might throw up their own lungs at any point. That left two as genuine dangers: one holding a blast-gun, and the fourth guard—a young woman—who's hand was hovering over her own energy pistol. She looked like she wanted to see if she could take me. She couldn't, but no one said that you had to be smart to be a guard.

We all stood there for a few seconds. Most of the guards tried to figure a way out of the situation, and one of them desperately wanted to make it worse.

She decided to make it worse.

Her hand touched the grip of the energy pistol in her holster, and the second she did, I drew my own and shot her in the head, hitting the blast gun user in the throat before he could fire his own weapon. They both went down, as the remaining two guards—one of whom was *still* desperately in need of medical attention—tried to look like they didn't know the dead guards and had never meant me any harm anyway.

I removed the medical pouch from my leg and tossed it over to the guards. "Get her help or she'll die," I told the young man who looked like he might throw up. He nodded continuously for several seconds before picking up the pouch and helping his dying friend.

I found the remains of the pilot, and after a quick search, removed the access card for the behemoth. "Where did Ekhar go?" I asked the two living guards.

"She ran," the male said without looking back at me as he treated his companion's wounds. "Left us to die."

"That's what cowards do," I told him. "Find somewhere safe for the day, Trias will be dead by tomorrow along with anyone who works for him."

"What if he kills you?" The guard asked me, looking back over his shoulder.

"Then you can tell whatever story you need to in order to make it sound like you survived against horrific odds. You'll be heroes. Or hide. Or run. I don't care." I turned away and pressed the access card against a small panel on the side of the behemoth's leg, which in turn dropped a ladder from the rear of the vehicle.

A quick climb, and I entered the cockpit. Taking a seat in the relatively comfortable chair, I retracted the ladder, sealing the cockpit off, and activating the systems in the behemoth. It didn't take long for me to reacclimatise myself with the workings of the vehicle—there are some things that you don't forget. I turned the monstrous metal contraption around to leave the forecourt, checking that the missiles and plasma chain-cannon were both operational.

The checks were about done when the behemoth's scanner started to beep about targets behind me, toward the entrance to the building. Behemoths weren't exactly the nimblest of war machines, but as I turned around to face whatever the scanners had picked up, my heart lurched into my mouth. There were dozens more creatures, most of them the armoured variety. Apparently, the scientists in the lab had made a blasted army of the things. I rested my hands on the controls either side of the pilot's chair.

The weapons armed.

The creatures roared and charged.

CHAPTER EIGHT

The plasma canons opened fire with the merest touch of my finger against the control pad. As I moved my hand slightly across the panel, the behemoth's arm followed suit. The plasma bolts that left the chain-cannon tore through everything in their path; creatures and building alike. Pieces of rubble and shattered glass cascaded over the corpses of the creatures and guards, creating their tomb.

Three quarters of the creatures had already moved out of the line of fire, so those hit were mostly the same type I'd been fighting earlier—unarmoured, clearly not as smart. Cannon fodder. If I hadn't been fighting for my life, I might have smiled at that one.

The larger creatures stayed back from the front lines, as though directing those ahead of them. Several of the non-armoured variety leapt up at the behemoth's legs. I took a few steps forward while continuing to fire on those who hadn't yet moved out of the way, squashing more than a few. I slammed my hand on the yellow button above the control panel, sending hundreds of thousands of volts through the exposed metal of the behemoth's legs. The smell of charred flesh and the screams of those who had been trying to climb toward me, filtered through the cockpit. I fought to get my initial disgust under control while continuing to fight.

Dozens of creatures lay dead, but more continued to flood from the front entrance of the building. I unleashed the missiles directly at the front of the building, which collapsed with a mighty rumble, killing dozens of the creatures as they tried to escape. I hoped that would at least slow their egress.

The plasma chain-cannon was rapidly running out of coolant to make sure it didn't explode. I did not want to be in the cockpit when that happened. More of the creatures—mostly of the armoured variety— were climbing up the behemoth now, the internal sensors screaming at me to do something about it. The panel next to the electroshock button said sixty-two percent. I just had to deal with it until it was ready.

Using one of the metal arms, I grabbed an armoured creature off the behemoth and squeezed the big metal hand shut until the monster popped like a balloon. I managed to grab two more and throw them at the baying crowd as the number of armoured creatures now outnumbered the weaker.

I controlled the behemoth to grab the plasma sword on its back, and ignited the blade, the bright green glow almost too much to look at directly as I swept it up in an arc that cut through everything in its path. The behemoth wasn't as fast as the creatures, but what it hit it killed, which was fine with me.

The sword came down on top of a group of armoured creatures all trying to get out of the way of one another. The blade almost vaporised some of them, and cleaved others in two.

The behemoth danced—as much as a ten tonne mech can dance—around the forecourt, cutting through anything that got too close, but the numbers were on their side, and soon there were too many grabbing hold of the behemoth's legs and I felt the mech buckle and fall.

The impact of the behemoth hitting the ground jarred through me, and I was thankful for the cockpit, as the glass flashed yellow. Whatever meagre shielding was in place did its job. Creatures swarmed over the mech, trying to smash into the cockpit. I waved the sword at them, but alarms tore through the cockpit as the creatures ripped into the sword arm of the behemoth, rendering it useless. I could initiate the repair systems, but that would stop the electroshock and I'd be completely helpless for the best part of a minute.

One of the creatures—a large, armoured variety with a dark

scar that ran over the armoured plates in a criss-cross pattern—stood on the glass of the cockpit, staring at me. Whatever humanity it had once held was gone, but it wasn't even an animal. Animals don't look at people with such hatred. This was something new. Something evil. This should never have been created, and I was not about to be killed by such monsters.

The electroshock panel said eighty-nine percent. Just a few more seconds, although as the creature reared up and brought down its front two hands... paws... whatever they were, onto the glass, the shield flickered. The creature repeated the action, and again the shield flickered yellow, although this time there was a slight hesitation.

Ninety percent.

The missile panel showed it was depleted, and the heated coils inside the behemoth would take even longer to recharge. The sword arm was useless, although still thankfully attached to the rest of the mech, and the chain-cannon was so close to overheating that it was as likely to kill me just as much as the creatures. That was my last option. If the glass broke, I'd detonate the rest of the chain-cannon ammo, killing everything around me, and myself. I wasn't about to be torn to pieces by things that shouldn't exist.

Ninety-one percent.

A watched electroshock panel never charges.

I used the behemoth's working arm to swipe across the front of the cockpit, but the creatures ran before it could connect, and leapt back on me as soon as it was safe. Alarms sounded again. More of the creatures were attacking the good arm just as more large, armoured creature scrambled back onto the cockpit and began trying to smash their way inside.

Ninety-six percent.

I was defenceless for the moment, could do nothing but watch as the creatures jumped up and down on the cockpit, the shields flaring with every impact. I scanned the panel for a shield percentage gauge but found nothing. *Superb.*

Ninety-nine percent.

The glass spider-webbed as fear jolted through me. My hand hovered over the control panel, ready to detonate the plasma chain-cannon. Ready to end my life, my chance to stop Trias. I could only hope that the message I'd sent off-world would do some good.

I took a deep breath as the electroshock panel beeped: *One hundred percent.*

The creatures smashed down once again, and a tiny piece of glass fell onto me as I hit the button for the electroshock. Anything on top of the behemoth died instantly. Repair systems initiated immediately as the mech got back to its feet. My sword lay on the ground, and the instant my missile arms came online, I picked up the sword, igniting the blade and stood ready to fight again.

There were maybe a dozen creatures left, but none of them wanted to get close enough. They'd just seen the behemoth kill dozens of their own kind, their smouldering bodies now littering the snowy ground. I maintained my guard and my heart soared as the chain-cannon arm came back online.

The missiles showed as being operational again and I fired them all at the creatures and surrounding area, destroying everything in their path, including a large chunk of the building, which crushed the remaining creatures. I had no way to tell if any of them had fled into the city, but the odds were that at least some had. They would be a problem for another day. I waited around as the repairs on the behemoth continued until both arms were no longer flashing red. The shield was still down though, no way to repair that without getting out and shutting everything down. The sword still worked, and I had one more barrage of missiles before it was completely exhausted.

It was a longer wait than I liked, but once the missiles were operational again, I fired them directly into the partially destroyed building, which collapsed—all but the tower I'd used remained standing. I'd made sure the other tower was part of the target and it fell onto the rest of the fuel depository, causing a large explosion somewhere deep inside of the facility. Good.

I kept watch on my handiwork, and when certain nothing

was about to flood out of the remains of the building, I turned the mech and ran out of the forecourt, through the gate as if it were made of paper, and down along snow covered streets toward Rika. The behemoth wasn't going to do much to help me fight Trias, but it would be a good gift as payment.

It wasn't a long run in the mech, and snowbanks were considerably easier to navigate, and I was grateful that I'd found a behemoth. The previous pilot hadn't even managed to get inside of it before those creatures had killed him, and I wondered at what point had Ekhar run for her life, leaving her allies to die. Probably the moment she realised she wasn't about to get what she wanted.

My thoughts turned to times before I'd come to Euria. I'd had a wife. A life. The civil war had changed all of that. I'd already been in the military when I'd met Lilia. She'd been a soldier in the Union navy, stationed above the planet of Vanestra, part of a large force who had gone there to help shore up the defences of a planet needed for shipping anything from food to medicine throughout Union space. The higher-ups hadn't considered just how badly the traitors wanted a win.

When the traitors arrived at Vanestra, the Union ships were outnumbered six to one, and Lilia's ship—a dreadnaught by the name of *Axe's Edge*—had been destroyed. All hands-on board lost. Several of the smaller ships in the area had suffered worse fates—disabled, boarded, and the enemy had tortured and murdered every living thing on them over the space of several weeks. The planet of Vanestra had been torn asunder.

Official figures indicated a loss at over twenty million, including on the planet and the ships above. The enemy had engaged in an arial bombardment using nebula scorchers; a weapon designed to destroy ships. Using them in an atmosphere was illegal. It was the first of many battles where the enemy used tactics the Union couldn't counter, couldn't foresee. Not until they started fighting back in similar ways, and by then you couldn't tell which side was meant to be the 'good guys'.

I left the Union during the war, came to Euria, hoping it was far enough away from everything, and that my hate and anger would be left behind too. I hated the enemy for killing the woman I loved, along with millions of other innocents. I hated the Union for doing nothing to combat the increasingly horrific tactics of those who wanted to eradicate us.

The hate and anger came with me to Euria but at least being so far away from the main combat let me hate in peace.

Arriving at Rika's place of business brought me back to my senses. I had things to do, and reminiscing wasn't one of them.

The shutter doors to Rika's business opened, and I ducked the mech down a little and took it into the workstation beyond. Dozens of Rika's trusted guards watched me, knowing full well that their rifles and energy pistols would do very little against a fully operational behemoth. Even if only I knew that *fully operational* was something this particular behemoth could no longer be classed as.

"That is a behemoth," Rika said as I opened the cockpit and climbed down.

"It's all yours," I told her.

"You brought me a gift of weaponry?" Rika asked. "Tell me again why we were never closer friends?"

"I'm a Blackcoat, you're a criminal."

"Ah, yes, a tale as old as time," Rika said sarcastically. "There is a lot of blood on this one."

"I found out what they were doing at the fuel depository," I said. "It was a front for some unpleasant science experiments."

"Those experiments are the cause of the damage?" she asked. "How likely are they to follow you here?"

"Not very," I admitted. "They're mostly smears under the fuel depository I dropped on them."

"Nicely done," Rika said with a nod of approval as she affectionally tapped one of the behemoth's legs, realised she had something on her hand, and wiped it on the chest armour of a guard stood close by.

"Is everything ready?" I asked her.

Rika nodded. "Is Ekhar dead?"

"No, she escaped," I admitted. "The others who grabbed me

are dead, her husband is in Trias' Spire as a prisoner, and I got the off-world message sent."

"So, hopefully that means The Wardens," Rika said, sounding anything but hopeful. The Wardens arriving would probably put a dampener in her work, but that couldn't be helped and she knew that. Better The Wardens disrupting things than Trias murdering anyone who stood in his way.

I walked with Rika out of the workshop as her people set about either dismantling or fixing the behemoth, it would depend on what would make them the most money.

The maze of corridors we walked ended in a large open room with several workbenches around its perimeter, and an extra-long workbench in the middle. The latter of which was piled high with gear.

"Ghillie cloak," Rika said, picking up the flimsy looking charcoal grey item before replacing it. The cloak itself turned invisible, but it also projected out in a wide enough range to ensure that my boots and weapons would be invisible too. No point in wearing the cloak if a sword bobbing in the air gave me away.

"Thermosuit," I said, pointing at the black and orange armour.

"Also, matching recon armour," Rika said.

The thermosuit would keep me alive traversing so high up in the air. I picked up the recon armour boots.

"They've got stealth tech built in," Rika said. "Footstep dampeners, and they sync with the ghillie cloak. You're going to be able to come and go as you please. The armour has a force shield installed, so you can take some fire against energy weapons, but don't make a habit of it. The shield won't last long, and recon armour isn't designed for a firefight."

I nodded. There was no point in telling her I knew about recon armour, or ghillie cloaks, or anything else for that matter. Rika would explain it anyway as if I was a new-born. It was her way of making sure her buyer knew what they were getting so it wasn't her fault if they screwed it up.

"Not a stealth suit?" I asked.

"Couldn't get one," Rika said. "So, we had to cobble together pieces to bastardise one. The recon armour for part one, the ghillie suit for part two, you also have climbing gloves and a breather. None of which are specifically designed to be used in a stealthy manner, but they should keep you alive and… mostly safe."

"*Mostly?*" I asked with a raised eyebrow.

"You're going to try and kill the most important person on the planet," Rika said. "*Mostly* is about as safe as I can get you."

She had a point.

"Weapons?" I asked.

"Keep your carbonate-fibre blade, you'll need that to kill Trias if you're too stupid to not shoot him in the head from a distance," Rika said, picking up a plasma blade, much like the one in the behemoth, although vastly smaller. She ignited the blue blade and swept it around in front of her in an expertly handled arc. The blade hummed with power. "Two of these. Two energy pistols—I see you managed to break one already—and that's it. You're going in light, and you're going in silent."

I picked up one of the silenced energy pistols. The barrel was slightly shorter, and because of the silenced coil, it meant less shots before it overheated, but it was an excellent weapon.

"Anything else?" I asked.

"Two plasma mines and two plasma grenades," Rika said. "Just in case. Like I said, you need to pack light. No rifles, nothing heavy or bulky. You're going to be at the mercy of the wind while you zip along something with the thickness of your little finger."

"Thank you for making it sound so normal and not at all terrifying," I said with a smile.

"You brought me a behemoth, you get the Grade A service," Rika replied. "Also, I want you to succeed. Not just because Trias is a tyrannical megalomaniac, or because he's going to screw around with my business, but he killed my brother. My brother and I weren't especially close, but he was still my brother. I loved him. I want Trias and his whole empire to burn for that."

"I'll do my best."

"I know," Rika said. "Get ready and then we'll go see the grapnel launcher."

"I assume it's no longer in pieces," I said hopefully.

"It's already on its way to the best spot in the district of rich assholes," Rika said. "It'll be on the roof when we get there. You have one shot at this."

I nodded. "I know."

"There's a sink in the room next to this one, go get washed up first. You might not get the chance to later."

"Thank you," I said, meaning it.

"See you outside," Rika said walked toward the exit, she paused in the doorway, and looked back at me. "Are those drugs out of your system?"

I nodded.

"You sure?"

"I feel fine," I said. "Eating seemed to stop whatever it was, and there's no dizziness or adverse effects. I'll take a med-test before I go."

"See that you do," Rika said and left the room.

I took my time getting ready, checking the ghillie cloak, armour, thermosuit, and weapons. I was pretty sure Rika wouldn't screw me over, and that she would only give me her best gear, but it was force of habit. I didn't go into combat without checking my own gear first. I'd known people who hadn't checked, and they were no longer around to complain about it.

When I was done, I went next door and stripped off, washing myself clean of any grime and muck that I'd acquired from my sojourn to the fuel depository. I left my armour on the bathroom floor and walked back to the room with my new gear inside, getting dressed and feeling good about the prospects of what came next.

I finished dressing, placing the energy pistols in the holsters at my hip, my carbonate-fibre dagger in the sheath against the small of my back. Each sword went into the sheaths against my back, one sword hilt protruding up from behind each shoulder. I practised drawing and replacing them until it was smooth. Same with the energy pistols.

When I was satisfied that I'd done all I could, I found a med-test in a nearby medical room. I placed my thumb on the recyclable white pad, and activated the small, orange device. The pin pricked me, and I waited a few seconds for the blood results, which came back negative. Happy to be proven right, and ready for what I was to face next, I went to find Rika.

CHAPTER NINE

The journey, in the back of a large truck with snow caterpillars for wheels, was done in silence. Rika sat beside me, constantly looking out of the thick, tinted windows as if worried about being followed. I wasn't quite as paranoid as she, and only stared out of the window every few seconds.

The closer we got to the Spire, we passed by the large accommodation towers that were meant to house thousands of people but in reality only housed hundreds, and only the wealthy. The Spire and its surrounding buildings were a playground for the wealthy and powerful, and it had been that way since I'd arrived on the planet. There were walkways between several of the buildings, but none between them and the Spire itself, just in case anyone got the idea that they were on the same level as Trias.

The Spire loomed over everything else by a vast amount, all glass and dark metal. Hundreds of stories high, and occupied by a heavily guarded Trias, along with his most loyal followers. There was a small army within. An army I hoped to bypass. The other option—having to go through them—wasn't worth thinking about.

The truck stopped and Rika got out first, flanked by her guards from the front and rear of the vehicle. Another truck sat parked up a short distance away, next to the entrance to one of the accommodation towers.

I looked up at the cloud of freezing mist overhead, hiding the tops of most of the towers from view. I did not want to have to climb through that if I didn't have to. I'd done an orbital jump through freezing fog once, and it had been the most terrifying experience of my life up until this point.

Rika motioned for me to follow her, which I did without comment. The wind was loud as it whipped around the massive accommodation structures, and I'd have had to shout to be heard. Better to just talk when inside somewhere warm.

Most of the two dozen guards who had accompanied us through the city remained with the vehicles. Rika, myself and two guards—one large man with dark skin and a bald head, and one almost as large woman with paler skin, but also a bald head—entered the building and we made our way to the elevators, the interiors of which were lined with mirrors on three of the four walls, with a polished wooden floor and matching ceiling. Only the door, which was painted in a swirl of yellows and greens, was made of metal.

Rika tapped the elevator control panel, and selected number two-hundred and one from the drop-down menu that appeared. That was a long way up, and while the elevators moved at an incredible speed, it still took several seconds for the doors to reopen.

The cold hit me immediately, and I was grateful I hadn't removed my face covering as I stepped out of the elevator into a long corridor with most of the floor in front of me still under construction. The main beams and struts had been in place, but the rest was a skeleton of metal and glass. At least the floor was done.

"Construction ceased," Rika said.

"Why?" I asked.

"The people in charge of it decided they wanted to be paid more," Rika said as we walked down the corridor, the place where the window should be at the end was nothing but an open void into the abyss outside.

"Trias had them removed," I said.

"From the top of the Spire," Rika said. "Turns out, having looked into the best place to put this damn grapnel, I learned a lot more about our leader than I ever wanted to know."

There were dark marks on the makeshift wooden floor. "You dragged it this way?" I asked.

"Put it on a trolley, actually," Rika said as we reached a partition that had been set up to create the room beyond.

The grapnel was being screwed into the exposed metal beams beneath it and hooked into the metal beams above. It wasn't going to get any more secure than that.

"It'll lift a behemoth," Rika said as the three workers stopped and nodded to her.

"It's ready," a young human woman said, her hair half shaved, leaving the other half long enough to reach her shoulders. She'd turned it bright pink. It was the little acts of self that made all the difference on a planet where everyone was meant to be working for the *greater good.*

"Thank you," Rika said. "All of you back down to the ground. Get in the vehicles. No one speaks of this. Ever."

"Yes, Rika," all three said at once before leaving us alone as Rika motioned for her guards to remain in the hallway.

Rika pointed outside of the hole where the corner of the building should be. "You see the Spire?" She asked.

I nodded. The fog wasn't so bad up here, and the buildings jutted out from it like ants leaving their nest. Dozens of looming steel and glass structures, with the Spire dwarfing them all.

Rika knelt behind the grapnel launcher to look through the attached scope. I was silent while she worked, and a loud bang signified the launcher being fired. The grapnel vanished into the distance, leaving the thin, but super-strong cable attached to the launcher as it trailed off into the distance.

"Take a look," Rika said, getting up.

I sat where she'd been and peered through the scope. The grapnel had attached itself to a large metal weather rod. Most of the buildings had them; they converted the lightning that hit it into electricity that helped power the buildings. The rod was twelve feet long and weighed about as much as a truck. The grapnel was going nowhere.

Rika unfolded a piece of parachute-like material from a bag beside her, and hooked it onto a carabiner that sat on the cable. The parachute drooped, hopefully cocooning me inside and keeping me still as I hurtled across the chasm. I'd used one before.

"Now or never," I said.

"I'm going to stay here and watch," Rika said. "When you're across, you're going to need to blast out one of the windows. Use the plasma mine, it'll cut through the glass over there like paper."

"Understood."

"You need to attach this to the grapnel," she continued, tossing me a device about the length of my forearm. There was a yellow handle one side with a grey switch beside it, and handholds on the other side. "These will burn out before you can get there and back."

I followed Rika's point to the device already attached to the cable.

"When you want to return, you'll need to climb back up to the cable, attach this new one, grab the handle on the device and flick the switch. It'll bring you back here at speed."

"A way out too," I said with a smile. "How thoughtful."

"I figured it's better than you dying in a blaze of glory, or however you envisaged going out."

"I didn't plan to die," I said. "I just thought it likely."

"Yeah, well, try not to die," Rika said nonchalantly. "I've become accustomed to having you around, and Prasan would only be waiting to haunt me in the afterlife should I die and didn't give you every chance to get free."

"With that expression of disappointment on his face?" I asked with a smile.

Rika laughed. "Damn, yes. That man's special talent was to make sure you knew he was upset at you without ever saying a damn word."

I laughed with Rika. "He was one of the good guys."

Rika's smile faltered a little. "I wish we'd spent more time together as adults. We followed different paths."

"He loved you," I told her. "He didn't always approve of what you did, or who you worked with, but he loved you. He was proud of you. I looked out for you too, made sure that if we heard anything about someone giving you or your people trouble, we'd look into it. He made it sound like he was just doing his job, but I knew it was his way of making sure you were safe."

Rika turned away and let out a deep breath. "Didn't ask for that."

"He knew," I said. I considered placing a hand on her shoulder for comfort, but Rika was more the touch without permission and lose a hand kind of person.

Rika turned back to me and sighed. "Thank you for being his friend. For standing by him."

"He was the one who found out about Trias," I said. "He came to me with it. He knew I wasn't on the take of Trias or his people. He wanted a fair society. He wanted people to do well no matter their station in life. He didn't believe in having power just because you were rich. Prasan felt power and influence should be earned through action and deed, not just because you had a rich daddy."

The bald male guard from the ride up the elevator entered the room, his expression suggesting he wouldn't have interrupted unless it was urgent.

"What's going on, Scios?" Rika asked.

"A whole lot of guards coming our way," he said. "I think they know we're here."

Rika looked over at me. "Plans change. I'm going to have to go help keep my people safe. You'll be okay getting across, yes?"

I nodded. I figured Trias would realise I'd be coming for him, so I expected some form of resistance once I got into the Spire. "I'm sorry," I said. "I didn't mean to bring you and your people into harm's way."

Rika hugged me tight, which took me by surprise. "Just make sure you kill the fucker," she said and sauntered out of the room with Scios right on her heels.

I stared at the grapnel launcher for several seconds, and then outside at the fog that obscured the ground several thousand feet below.

I placed the spare device in one of the pouches against my leg, and sat myself into the parachute material, wiggling up until my head was at one end, and my feet at the other. Taking hold of the handle above me, I made sure my grip was tight before I took a deep breath, activated my ghillie cloak, watching on as I became almost invisible, then flicked the switch.

The velocity took my breath away, and I was grateful the parachute ensured I couldn't see below me as I rocketed along the hundreds of feet between the two buildings.

I concentrated on my breathing, making sure to slowly count with each breath. I wasn't particularly bothered by heights, which seeing how I used to jump from the orbit of planets is probably a good thing, but I didn't particularly like not being in control. And hurtling along a finger-sized cable at high speed certainly came under the headline of *not in control*.

I craned my neck to get a look at how close I was to my destination, realised I was much closer than I thought I'd be and braced for impact as I hit the buffer on the grapnel side of the line. The parachute swayed violently from side to side, but I kept calm until it stopped. Only then did I remove my hands from the device and grab hold of the weather rod, pulling myself out of the parachute as I twisted around. There was a heart-in-mouth moment as my feet dangled over nothing, until they were safety behind the rod on the ledge of the building.

The ledge itself was much larger than I'd expected, and at nearly four feet in width, would make traversing it an easier prospect than I'd prepared for. Finally, a little good news. Gripping the weather rod as tightly as possible, I reached out, grabbing the parachute and pulling it toward me, unclipping it as it moved. A gust of wind caught the chute and threatened to yank it from my hand, but it only lasted a second before it was safely being folded up.

I took a moment on the ledge to look around. The device I'd used to speed along the grapnel line was smoking, and moments later there was a click and it simply fell apart, tumbling down into the darkness below. Good job I'd gotten off when I had.

I walked along the ledge and found a large window to a small, empty room. The plasma mine stuck immediately against the window, and I tapped the activation button on top of the mine twice, then moved away as quickly as I could as the mine did its job.

Plasma mines activate by pushing out a circle of plasma in a three-foot radius. It's designed to remove legs and feet, not outright kill people, although you can get ones that bounce in the air before performing the same action.

The plasma mine fizzled out, leaving a large hole in the window for me to climb through and almost immediately be grateful that I was standing on solid ground once again.

There was nothing of interest in the sparse room, and I made my way to the door, carefully pulling it open a fraction to peek into the hallway beyond. I was wearing my ghillie cloak, so I was pretty much invisible, but doors don't open by themselves.

The walls were unpainted; no carpet or floor covering of any kind, and no doors on any of the rooms. I stepped into the hallway, wondering what was going on, but as I made my way along, peering into each doorless room, I noted that none of the rooms were decorated. They were all apartment sized, but they were completely empty. Each a large open space that could fit an entire family, and Trias and his rich friends just left them empty instead of allowing anyone without wealth to live in them. What a waste.

At the far end of the winding hallway was the only door on the floor, but there was no security lock, nothing like I'd expect to find. The lights above flickered and went off, leaving me in darkness. "Trias lives in a shithole," I muttered as I pushed open the door and stepped into the stairwell.

I ran up the stairs, the boots absorbing the sound I made. I ignored more doors until I came to the end of the stairwell several flights up. The only way to get to the penthouse, and Trias, was to access the penthouse-only elevator at the opposite end of the floor I'd reached. Before Prasan and I had been targeted by Trias' people, we'd discussed ways to get to Trias and stop him. The building blueprints had been easy enough to acquire, although I wondered if that small act had been the thing that had finally set Trias against us.

I drew a plasma blade, pushed open the door just enough to

squeeze through, and stepped inside. My ghillie cloak ensured the three guards at the far end of the hallway didn't react as I made sure the door closed slowly.

The guards were sat around a table in front of a large window playing some kind of card game, and I took my time as I walked along the hallway—this one with carpeted floors. There were three doors along the hall, each one leading to a large room. I remembered them from the blueprints, although the plans had also suggested everything was going to be decorated to a high specification, so I guessed they could have been wrong.

I was halfway down the hallway when one of the doors opened and a fourth guard stepped out. She looked down the hallway toward the three men playing cards and waved. Two of them waved back. I froze in place. Although I was invisible, it wasn't a hundred percent effective. The ghillie cloak bent the light around me, making me look like I wasn't there at a glance, but if you stared for too long, you often saw the outline of something, or the brain registered that something wasn't entirely right. The latter of which appeared to be happening to the female guard, who stared directly at me for what felt like an eternity.

I'd hoped to get through the floor to the elevator and up to the penthouse without having to fight my way and alert everyone above. As the guard's hand reached for the energy pistol at her hip, I knew that was no longer an option.

I rushed forward and ignited the plasma sword, the humming blue blade was unable to be completely concealed by the energy field the ghillie suit gave off. It looked like a light blue blur and, judging from the look of confusion on the guard's face, it was something she hadn't seen before.

As I ran, the ghillie suit couldn't keep up with my movements and began to falter.

"Ghillie..." the woman started before I plunged the blade up into her throat, twisting it and removing it from the side of her neck in one movement as I sprinted on toward the card players at the end of the hallway.

I moved beyond her falling body, ignoring the open door, as

the three men all got up from their table at once, showering the cards and chips over the floor as they went for their weapons.

As I ran, I drew the second plasma blade from its sheath, reaching the closest guard before he'd drawn his pistol. My plasma blade cut through his side just below his ribs, exiting the other side as if slicing through air.

The second guard had his gun out, but I brought both plasma swords down in an arc, catching him in the top of his shoulder, and dragging the blades through his body and out his ribcage on the opposite side. I kicked him in the chest, sending him sprawling into the third guard, who fired twice, hitting me in the shoulder and disengaging the ghillie suit, which flickered as I drove both blades into his heart.

I returned the swords to their sheaths and searched the area for any alarms that might have been triggered, and I found a small button on the side of the wall beside where the guards had been playing. *Damn it.* I guessed the stealthy option was out.

The hallway was now covered in blood, so it wasn't as if I'd been able to remain in stealth-mode forever, but the knowledge that it was only going to get tougher from here out still annoyed me.

The flickering ghillie suit was all but useless now, so I tossed it to the floor before searching the rooms for anything that might prove useful. They were empty of people, and appeared to be designed to keep the guards occupied while on duty. A small kitchen sat behind one door, and several of the large rooms contained beds.

I searched the dead guards and found an elevator control card on the female guard. With a deep breath, I unsheathed one of the plasma blades again and headed over to the elevator, called one of them to me, and stepped inside when it arrived. The control card beeped against the security panel inside the glass-walled elevator, the doors closing a moment later.

Time to finish this.

CHAPTER TEN

The elevator opened in a barrage of gun fire, destroying the glass and punching holes in the metal of the elevator itself. Thankfully, I wasn't in the elevator.

The moment the doors had closed, I'd used my plasma blades to cut a hole in the ceiling and hoisted myself onto the roof. Once inside the elevator shaft, I'd quickly climbed up the nearby ladder and moved along the lattice-covered metal floor and down the next ladder to the other elevator car. I'd cut through the roof of that one, and set it to go up to the penthouse floor, and then climbed out again and waited.

When the first elevator had arrived and the guards waiting had opened fire without thinking, I'd dropped down from the roof of the next car along, and stepped through the open door, flinging a plasma grenade at the congregating group of guards.

The grenade exploded, vaporising large parts of anyone unlucky enough to be in the blast radius. Screams and gurgles of pain filled the hallway that had once been painted in a pastel yellow but was now mostly splattered in blood and gore. The control panel to the elevators was, thankfully, destroyed. The doors were trying to close, but were unable to, rendering both elevator cars useless. A little bit of luck on a day when I needed it.

I walked past the remains, ending two guards who were still alive but were never going to last long considering the damage the grenade had done to them. They probably deserved to suffer a little longer, but I wasn't beyond offering mercy to those who needed it. As I walked on down the hallway, I wondered if I'd offer that same mercy to Trias. No, probably not.

The first door I reached burst open and a guard ran out, almost barrelling into me. I twisted aside and plunged one of the plasma swords up into his throat, pushing him away as I drew my second sword to parry the dagger of the guard coming to join his friend.

The man stepped back and drew an energy gun, firing at where I'd been a moment ago. I dropped one sword, drew the energy pistol and shot the guard in the chest as he ran after me. His armour stopped it, but it let me step inside his defence and plunge the plasma sword I still held into his heart, cutting through his armour with ease.

After checking I wasn't about to be attacked again, I gathered my second plasma sword and resheathed it. Inside the dingy, windowless room was a man strapped to a chair. His feet were in a bowl of water that had ice crystals forming on it. He was naked and covered in cuts and bruises. Ekhar's husband. He'd been given a long, hard death for her failures. I wondered where she was, did she have a similar fate? Did Trias execute her? Did he make her watch as her loved one was brutalised?

I bowed my head slightly as a mark of respect for the dead and muttered, "May the stars take you." It was an old gesture that I'd picked up during my time in the Union military. I didn't know if he was involved in what his wife had been doing, but I was pretty sure he didn't deserve to die the way he had.

I left the room and took a deep breath. The huge, ornately carved door at the end of the hallway lead to Trias' personal quarters. Forty feet between me and a chance of redemption, of justice. Vengeance. Plasma blade gripped tight in my hand, I set off.

There were three more doors between me and Trias. One was open, and I peered inside at the large, but mostly empty room that held several bunks and a few tables. A place for the guards to rest, away from Trias but close enough to be there when needed.

I tried the next door along, which had a second door further inside the room, and immediately wished I hadn't opened it. Blood drenched every part of the small room, and pieces of bodies were strewn around. I spotted a head and arm, but most of the rest was just unidentifiable meat.

I drew my second plasma blade from its sheath, igniting it, feeling a little better for the accompanying hum. I closed the door and scanned the hallway, a feeling of unease filling me. At the last door, I really didn't want to open it but knew I needed to make sure I wasn't about to be ambushed. I toed the door open.

The room inside was entirely made of metal. Chains hung from the ceiling, and more adorned the floor. It smelled like sweat and blood, and I had no interest in stepping inside. *A torture chamber.* I closed the door, moved further down the hall, wanting everything over as soon as possible.

Trias' door had no security panel or even a handle to stop people from coming and going. Again, I nudged it slightly ajar with my foot. Only darkness.

"You've killed a lot of my people." Trias' voice came from within that darkness. "I thought I'd just leave the door unlocked for you since you want to see me so much."

I pushed the door all the way, until it clicked in place, and did the same with the adjacent door, allowing in a small amount of light from the hallway, but not enough do much for the pitch black beyond.

"You're a coward," I said stepping into the room and edging to the side, letting my eyes adjust to the darkness. The light from the hallway would frame me and make me an easy target.

"No, I'm just not going to fight you in the open," Trias said. "You have become a thorn in my operation, Celine Moro. You have killed my people, you have eluded capture, and have conspired against me from the very beginning. I killed your partner because I thought he was the greater threat. I was wrong."

"I've contacted The Wardens," I said, trying to pinpoint Trias' voice. "They'll be coming for you."

"And I will have a story ready for them about how a disgruntled Blackcoat murdered her own partner and came after me because of your delusions brought on by your time in the war."

I was a little surprised at that.

"Your silence means you didn't think I'd discover your past," Trias said. "To be honest, I should have done so many weeks ago, but I left it to others to deduce. They were useless. I believe you found their remains in the room along the hallway. I do not believe that those who fail to do their jobs should be given a third chance. Once is a mistake. Twice is a pattern."

"Are you going to talk me to death?"

"No," Trias said. "I just wanted you to know that your efforts were for nothing. Your friends will die, your name will be removed from the records. It will be as though you never existed. You saw Ekhar's husband, yes? She failed me twice; I had a different plan for her though."

"You throw her out of the window or something?" I asked before I could stop myself.

"Kill her," Trias said.

The roar bounced around inside the darkness, making the hair on the back of my neck stand on end, and causing my heart to race. I didn't want to believe what was in front of me. No one deserved that. I moved back toward the entrance to the room as the sound of crashing footsteps started toward me. They quickened in pace and before I reached the doorway, I was hit from the side, and slammed into the wall, the breath knocked out of me. Something grabbed my leg, lifting me off the ground, and I slashed up at the creature who had hold of me. It screamed and threw me away. I tumbled down the hallway, coming to a stop close to the room that held Ekhar's dead husband.

I looked up from my position on the floor as the creature came through the doorway, having to duck down to do so. It was twelve feet tall, and almost as wide, with dark pink flesh covering its entire body. It wore the tatted remains of black trousers, but nothing else. Long, dark red hair cascaded down a face that no longer looked human. Mandibles jutted from the remains of their mouth, clacking together as it stalked toward me. One hand was now just a large red claw, and the other had elongated pink fingers, that got darker toward the tip. A large cut bled across the wrist of the hand with fingers, presumably where I'd caught it with my plasma sword.

"Ekhar," I whispered.

The creature stopped walking and screamed at me. Whatever remained of Ekhar remembered who she used to be, remembered me. Blamed me. The creature's large red eyes narrowed.

It charged.

I jumped to my feet, ignited both plasma blades, and stood my ground. The creature that used to be Ekhar swiped down at me with her clawed hand and I launched myself back, slicing at it with one plasma blade, trying to cut through the thick skin that wrapped around the arms.

Ekhar moved faster than I'd expected and grabbed my arm as the blade passed by. She wrenched me off my feet and threw me into the ceiling, which I brought down with me as I hit the hallway floor. One of the plasma blades skittered out of my grasp as Ekhar kicked me in the ribs, sending me spiralling along the hallway, back toward Trias' apartment.

I drew one energy pistol and fired twice at Ekhar, who raised her arms to deflect the shot. She was too well armoured to hurt with such relatively weak weaponry. I set the overload function, waited for Ekhar to get close enough that I could feel her fetid breath on me, but before I could fire at her chest, she moved, and I inwardly cursed her speed and agility for something so massive. Her claw racked along the armour around my ribs, ripping through it, and drawing a pain-filled yell from me.

I twisted my body, avoiding the fist that would have shattered my legs, and fired the overload directly into Ekhar's shoulder. Flesh sizzled, filling my nostrils as the blast took Ekhar's claw arm clean off, leaving nothing but a jagged, leaking wound. She screamed at me, grabbed my leg and almost casually slammed me against the wall, before doing the same against the other side of the hallway. My vision darkened when my head bounced off the wall, and she tossed me back down the hallway. She was toying with me, enjoying it. She picked up her own arm and laughed. I watched in dazed horror as her arm began to regenerate.

I sighed, and got painfully to my feet, reignited the plasma blade but left my energy pistol holstered for now. I took a deep breath. "Come get me, you bastard."

Ekhar charged. I let her get close enough and rolled under her attempt to grab me, slashing through her knee and thigh with my plasma sword, and getting to my feet close to her back. I punched the plasma sword into where her ribs would be and ignored the scream of pain as I twisted it and dragged it out, leaving a gaping wound in her side that oozed black blood.

I dodged another swipe, removed the plasma mine from the small of my back and slammed it into the wound, igniting it and throwing myself back, rolling down the hallway to get as far from the ignition as I could.

Ekhar tried to get her fingers inside the wound, but it was too late. The mine exploded. The impact bisected her right across the hips, and her entire upper body collapsed forward as if she were an old building being demolished.

I gingerly got to my feet and leaned up against the wall. My body hurt. My armour was all but ruined from the impact of the claw, and I could feel blood trickling down my skin in too many places to count. I was not in good shape, but at least I wasn't split in half from a mine, so I had that going for me.

Using the wall for aid, I made my way back along the hallway toward Trias and the hopeful end of everything. When I reached the remains of Ekhar, the mandibles on her face clicked at me, trying to grab my legs. How was she still alive?

I jumped away as one arm slowly swiped toward me. The pink flesh of both halves of her body was now a deep burned charcoal, but still, she tried to drag herself toward me.

"You don't know when to quit, do you?" I asked, removing a plasma grenade from my belt. I punched the plasma sword down through the top of Ekhar's head, pinning her under the jaw to the hallway floor. I released the sword and pulled one of her mandibles aside, activated the plasma grenade, and shoved it in her mouth.

I turned and ran toward Trias' still open doors as the grenade detonated. If Ekhar survived that, she probably deserved to live on, especially considering I didn't have anything else that would do that level of damage. I left the plasma sword where it was, just in case, and picked up the one that I'd dropped earlier, activating it and walking on toward Trias' penthouse.

Drawing my remaining energy pistol, I stepped into the dark penthouse, half expecting to be shot at or attacked from the darkness, but there was nothing. I moved to the side of the room and found the lighting controls on the wall, activating them to reveal the massive disc-shaped room.

There was a large circular sofa in the middle of the room that surrounded a large wooden table. Several tables and chairs were positioned around the outside of the room. One hallway sat directly opposite the entrance, and I ran over to it, staying to one side as I felt a cold breeze reach me.

When I was certain it was safe—as safe as could be—I continued down the hallway, ignoring the half dozen doors that led to different parts of the penthouse as the repeated bang of a door drew all my attention.

At the end of the snaking hallway was a large metal door that hadn't been quite shut when someone had gone through it. Snow filtered through the gap, and I pushed it open, my pistol ready to fire on anyone behind it. All I found were steps leading to the roof of the Spire, the wind howling above.

I took the steps slowly, not wanting to poke my head out the top and make myself a target, but the room contained only Trias, sat cross-legged in the middle, watching as I raised my gun and fired.

When Trias was running for the position of Councillor, he had a video prepared that showed him fighting. Someone had told him that it made him look dangerous, like someone who could take care of himself and his people. They'd lied; I thought he looked like someone playing at fighting. Trias wasn't a trained soldier, he was an administrator, but he was still dangerous.

The energy blast hit the energy shield in front of Trias' head and dissipated. "That the best you can do?" he asked as the wind died down.

"You do that?" I asked, surprised I could hear him.

"This roof is fitted with sound dampeners," he told me, getting to his feet. "Heated floors too. It's useful when I need to take off and land. I figured killing you up here was more poetic. Also, I didn't want to ruin the upholstery in my apartment any more than you've already done."

"I'm sorry about that," I said. "Turns out you just hire people who bleed a lot."

Trias expression darkened. "I'm going to enjoy this."

"I guarantee you won't," I said, and shot him twice in the chest, continuing to shoot as I ran toward him while he used his shield to block the shots. I dropped my plasma blade in preparation to unsheathe the carbonate-fibre dagger, but Trias ran at me, shocking me, as he took the offensive. His shield slammed into me, knocking me off my feet, and I dropped the pistol.

Trias kicked the energy pistol off the side of the building as I got to my knees, and his shield punched out again, smashing into me and pinning me to the ground, the green tinted shield wrapping around me, squeezing me.

"It's amazing that people think I can only use this power for defence," Trias said as he stood above me. He kicked me in the face, breaking my nose. Blood gushed down my face, spreading over the sides of my cheeks.

Trias grabbed me by the hair and dragged me upright, before continuing across the rooftop. I kicked and twisted, but his shield tightened around me, pinning my legs. He stopped when we were ten feet from the edge, forced me to look out over the frozen fog. The peaks of other buildings punched up as if trying to catch up to the mighty Spire.

"They tell me it's a long time before you hit the ground," Trias said, jutting his face to a few inches from mine—his breath reeked of alcohol. I'd interrupted him enjoying himself. Good. "When you're dead, I'm going to find everyone who helped you, and I'm going to turn them into more Ekhar's. They're going to be my pets."

His shield loosened a little, and he smiled, watching the panic in my eyes. With my arm free, I grabbed my carbonate-fibre dagger and drove it up toward Trias' stomach. He caught my wrist in one hand, his eyes wide—the dagger tip had gone through the shield he'd created.

"Did you think that was going to do it?" he screamed in my face. "Did you think you would win that easily?"

"No," I said, opening my left hand and letting the dagger fall. I caught it with my right and plunged it into Trias' thigh, ripping down toward his knee as he screamed in pain.

The shield gone, his blood poured out over the rooftop as he released me. I moved around the bastard, stabbing him over and over: side, back, shoulder, hip. He tried to push me away, but I swung up under his arm, and stabbed him in the armpit, twisting the blade. It hit bone, and I tore the blade out of his body by his shoulder.

Blood pumped from the wound, flooding over the rooftop.

"You talk too much," I said, spitting my own blood onto the floor. I was much more seriously hurt than I'd wanted to admit. Ekhar's monstrous form had done serious damage to my ribs and side, and I was having trouble breathing.

"I *own* this planet," Trias said, his words almost a plea. "I *own* all of you."

"I'm not for purchase," I said and slammed the dagger into his throat, cutting it wide open and pushing him onto the ground as I fell back hard, the jolt shooting up my spine.

I didn't know how long I sat there, but I saw a dark spot in the clouds to the north and knew that someone was coming for me. Trias was dead. I was dying. Everything was done. I discarded the dagger, lay back on the warm rooftop and looked across the sky at the mountains as the sun broke through.

As far as last days go, it could have been worse.

CHAPTER ELEVEN

The first thing I realised when I opened my eyes was that I wasn't dead. It took my brain a few seconds for that particular piece of information to marinate before I accepted it. The second thing was that I wasn't in a prison cell.

I was on a comfortable bed with what appeared to be clean sheets and a big fluffy pillow. There was a monitor beside me that beeped in time with my heart. It was connected to the bed, which monitored all of my vitals. They used them in the military and in most hospitals throughout the Union.

I sat up, decided my head didn't like that very much, and immediately lay back down until the world stopped spinning.

When everything went back to some semblance of normalcy, I examined the room. I was the only occupant. There were two doors, one was slightly ajar revealing a bathroom. The other was, I presumed, the exit. A yellow leather chair sat in one corner next to a small wooden table. There were three large windows directly behind my head, although I didn't dare sit up and turn around to get a look at the view.

The door opened and a woman of around fifty walked in. She had short greying hair, hazel eyes, and dark skin. A red and blue tattoo adorned her forearm. *Ex-military*. She wore a short-sleeved set of combat amour and had an energy pistol against each hip, and two daggers sat on a belt in front.

She took the yellow chair and placed it beside my bed. "My name is Andreous."

"You're a Warden," I said, noticing the star shaped badge that hung on a chain around her neck. The badge was made of carbonate-fibre too and could be used as a weapon should the need arise.

"I am," Andreous said. "We arrived about thirty seconds after a group of guards sent by Trias' allies touched down on the roof. They were going to pitch you off the side of it, or keep you hostage, or, who knows. They were bad people. They didn't surrender when asked, and now they're dead bad people."

"Good."

"Thought you'd like that," Andreous said with a smile. "We got your message. Actually, we were already here investigating Trias. We knew he was corrupt, but we didn't know everything, so that really helped."

"How long was I out?"

"Three months," Andreous said. "You were pretty close to being dead at one point; you'd lost a lot of blood, punctured lung, broken ribs, broken nose, skull fracture. In short you weren't going to be partying any time soon. You were completely healed up within a few weeks of being here, but we needed to know *exactly* what you'd discovered, so we put you in stasis. Didn't want anyone deciding to eliminate you while we took the evidence to the Council, and we weren't convinced we could trust you. You left a lot of dead people in your wake."

"Good," I said again.

Andreous chuckled. "They deserved to die, I know. The list of crimes we have against Trias and his people could fill a data-pad. You do thorough work."

"Thank you," I said, my throat scratchy. "Can I have a drink?"

Andreous nodded and filled a glass with water from the bathroom, helping me sit up, before letting me drink it.

"Better?" she asked when I was done.

I nodded. "Stasis sickness sucks."

"It does, but we also had another reason for putting you in stasis," she said. "You're not on Euria anymore. We had to take you to Atharoth, wasn't sure you'd be okay with going through the distance, so..." She shrugged.

"We're in Atharoth?" I asked, looking out the window for the first time at the city of Croleni. The birthplace of the Union. "I've never been here."

"Not many Orbital Shock Troopers get the opportunity," Andreous said.

"You know?"

"I'm a Warden," Andreous told me as if that explained it all, although thinking about it, it did. They had access to everything. There was very little hidden from a Warden.

"Why am I here?"

"Well," Andreous started, leaning back in the chair. "We brought your evidence to the Council, which, I have to tell you, was a lot of fun. Seeing all of those Councillors shit themselves when they realised we had Trias, was entertaining. They removed him as a member; I know he's dead, but his name will be stricken from the record now."

"What happened to Rika?" I asked, my brain catching up with what was happening.

"Ah, well, she arrived at Blackcoat headquarters with a small army, and we told her that you were fine and that she might want to sort out some kind of leadership as they were all dead or imprisoned. We left Rika and her people to deal with it. I think the planet might be undergoing some changes. There's a group of Wardens there to help out. They'll be fine. She told me to tell you that you owe her, but thank you. She seemed genuinely upset that you were hurt."

"She's a good person," I said. "Actually, she's a pain in the ass, but she does give a shit about the people in Euria so that's a start."

"More than Trias ever did," Andreous said. "We also found the remains of some interesting creatures. We'll be investigating further, something I thought you might like to help us with, considering the matter is still ongoing, and still linked to several sitting Councillors."

"Wait, what?" I asked, not sure if I'd heard correctly, or if my brain was just being weird again.

"Well, we brought you to Croleni because that's where Wardens are given their duty."

I stared at Andreous for several seconds. "You want me to be a Warden?" I asked eventually.

Andreous nodded. "Yes. You're ex-Orbital Shock Trooper, ex-Blackcoat. You took down a corrupt Councillor of the Union almost single-handedly, giving us enough evidence to arrest and remove half the politicians on Euria in the process. The Wardens are protectors of the Union. We investigate those in power who use that power given to them by the Union to make themselves better off at the expense of their own people. We protect the Councillors, their families, their staff, and do the same with the Royal Family. Sometimes people are elected to office and forget that they're there to make sure they help people; they just want money and power. We're there to make sure they don't stay in office long. Being a Warden is a long, hard job. It's—"

"Yes," I said, interrupting her. "Sorry, you were saying something."

Andreous laughed. "It's fine. There will be an official meeting where you'll get your badge, your Warden credentials, and anything else you need. And then we're going to hunt down every single Councillor who helped create those monsters on Euria." She offered me her hand, which I immediately took. "Welcome to The Wardens," Andreous said. "You ready to change things for the better?"

My smile threatened to get so wide I was certain it would never go away. "Lead the way," I told her, my grin widening again. "Time to go monster hunting."

ACKNOWLEDGEMENT

As always, writing is not as solitary an occupation as you might think, and a lot of people are involved in getting a book to publishing standard.

A big thank you to my wife, Vanessa, and our three daughters, Keira, Faith, and Harley. They've been a constant source of support over the years, and I couldn't have done this without them.

To my agent Paul Lucas for being supportive, helpful, and just all around awesome.

To Amanda J Spedding, my editor, who helped turn my words into something readable. It's always a pleasure to work with you and I hope to do so in the future.

A huge thank you to Wendy Saber Core for doing such an incredible cover for Blackcoat. It's almost exactly what I had in my mind, which isn't something that I often get to say about covers.

To my friends and family, and everyone who has been behind me the whole way, thank you. After the last few years of being more than a little shite, it's good to know that you have people who love and support you, and who are there for you when you need to complain about something.

A massive thank you to Sarah who has, over the years, beta read about half a dozen of my books, at least 3 or 4 or which haven't been published yet. Her input is always valuable, and she helps make the story better.

And so, we make it to the end of the first ever book I've published outside of the Hellequin universe. If you picked it up despite being a new genre and new world, thank you, I hope you enjoyed it as much as I enjoyed writing it.

And that's the end of the Blackcoat. It was a story that I've had on my hard drive for a few years now, just not doing anything and I figured that I may as well polish it up and let people read it. I hope you enjoyed it. Right now, it's a one off, but if it does well, and people want more, I'm sure I can find new stories for Celine and the world she lives in.

About the Author

Steve McHugh is an Award nominated, bestselling fantasy author. 13 books published and counting. Father of 3 daughters. Owner of epic backlog of videogames.

Blog: https://stevejmchugh.wordpress.com/
Twitter: https://twitter.com/StevejMchugh
Facebook: https://www.facebook.com/steveJMchugh
Amazon: https://amzn.to/2BYLi72

BONUS

If you enjoyed Blackcoat, here's the beginning of Frozen Rage, a novella set within the Urban Fantasy series, the Hellequin Chronicles and is a part of that series. It's available to purchase now.

The Realm of Dreich is a getaway for the rich and powerful, a medieval-inspired town in the middle of a vast frozen wilderness. Now it's the site of a wedding, intended to join two feuding families who have spent centuries in an uneasy truce with each other.

When Tommy Carpenter asks his best friend, Nate Garrett, to help him with the security of the wedding, Nate reluctantly agrees, knowing that it will be a long weekend of work and, in all probability, treachery.

It is only a matter of time before members of each family are found murdered and it is up to Nate and Tommy to find the killer before more bodies fall, potentially reigniting a war.

CHAPTER ONE

The Realm of Dreich.

I was pretty sure I'd made a terrible decision to come here.

"No, fuck you," the large man bellowed, getting to his feet at one end of the table laden with food and drink. He pointed a long finger at the man sat the opposite end, thirty feet away. If I was honest, it could have been three times that, and it still wouldn't have been long enough.

Tommy Carpenter, my best friend, stood beside me and sighed as he stroked his long, dark beard. A sure sign he was beginning to lose his patience. "I really wish I'd stayed at home," he muttered under his breath.

Thirty people sat around a table designed for twice that number, although the shouting match between the two men at the opposing ends had everyone else move back from where they'd been seated.

The hall we were in was designed to look like something from a European palace, with high ceilings where murals of various gods—some of whom I couldn't have named if I'd tried—

looked like they'd stepped off the pages of a fashion magazine. The walls were adorned with paintings, several of which I was almost sure were from masters of the craft back on the Earth Realm. At least one was an original Michelangelo, and I wondered from where they'd been stolen. The stained-glass windows that ran along one wall let in rainbows of color that bounced off the highly polished wooden floor.

"It's fucking Shakespearean," Remy said from the other side of me. "Maybe they'll murder one another, and we could all stop pretending we care."

As far as ideas went, it wasn't the worst I'd heard recently.

"Well, it is a wedding," Diana said from the other side of Remy. "It's probably not a proper wedding until at least one person has been bludgeoned with something."

"You go to some weird ass weddings," Remy said, looking up at her.

Remy was a three-and-a-half-foot tall fox-man. He'd pissed off the wrong witch coven, and they'd tried to kill him by turning him into a fox. Clearly, it hadn't worked but the witches had all died, and their lives had been poured into a newly fox-man shaped Remy. He dealt with it by swearing and threatening to stab people. To be honest, as far as coping mechanisms went, I'd heard worse.

The two men were now face to face, spewing insults about each other's mothers, fathers, and at one point a particularly inventive curse about a goat and a block of cheese.

"When do we step in?" Diana asked.

Tommy sighed. Like half the people sat at the table, he was a werewolf, although he was probably stronger than any of them, and certainly less likely to pick a fight at a wedding brunch with the father of the bride.

Werelions made up the other half of the guests. There was a long and unpleasant history between the two species, mostly involving vast numbers of murders. Peace had been brokered for a few centuries but that hadn't stopped either side trying to tear the other in half whenever the chance arose. Some don't forgive or forget, and some are just arseholes. The father of the bride and uncle of the groom most certainly fell into those categories.

An apple was thrown, and it smashed against the wall beside Diana's head. Diana hadn't even flinched, she just slowly turned to look at the remains of the destroyed fruit, and then back at the no longer arguing families. All eyes rested on her.

Diana was half werebear, and not someone you wanted to anger unless you liked the idea of having your arms ripped off so she could beat you to death with them.

My mind cycled through options of what was going to happen next when I spotted the expression of glee on Remy's face.

The doors to the dining hall were thrown open. "Enough," a large man bellowed as he stormed inside. He had a dark bushy beard, was broad shouldered with bulging muscles on his arms, and a barrel chest. Long, dark hair flowed over his shoulders. He couldn't have looked less like the romanticized version of a Viking if he'd been pulled into the room while standing on a long boat.

"I'm going outside," I said. "Come get me if they start to throw anything more dangerous than fruit."

Tommy clapped me on the shoulder, and I left through a side exit usually reserved for the staff. The castle was on theme with the dining hall, designed to resemble something from the Middle Ages, if not earlier, but it was a much more modern piece of architecture. Even so, there were several secret passages for staff to use, and on more than one occasion as I walked the long hallway—adorned with old water color paintings of wars, and a carpet that I was pretty sure was thick enough to lose yourself in if you stood still for too long—one of the larger paintings was pushed open and several members of staff emerged. Most wore an expression of *oh crap* on their face as they presumably tried to remember if I was one of the arseholes fighting in the dining hall.

As I exited the castle, nodding to the two guards directly outside the main entrance, I walked through the large courtyard to the sound of horses neighing in the distance. It had been snowing on and off for the twelve hours since I'd arrived in the realm, and while there were runes inscribed in the stone exterior of the castle to ensure the snow never built too high, there was still a satisfying crunch where my thick boots punched through the soft layer.

A large granite water feature sat in the center of the courtyard, depicting a sword in the stone. Water bubbled from the sword hilt, streaming down into a bowl beneath the statue. I smiled as I walked past. I'd seen Excalibur many centuries earlier, before it was lost, and I don't remember its hilt being quite so bejeweled.

After the courtyard, where there were more guards, I headed through part of a small village that encircled the castle and separated the makeshift from the real. The village, like the castle, had been purposefully-built, although the people who lived here were the workers and caretakers, so in that respect it was a real working village. But it was still designed to look hundreds of years older than it actually was. The village was surrounded by a forty-foot high, grey stone wall. The only way out was through the portcullis and across the drawbridge. As I strolled beneath the portcullis and across the dark wooden bridge, I noticed the crystal-clear water that made up the moat wasn't particularly deep, yet it was all part of the facade of the place.

At the end of the drawbridge, was a huge stone archway, and I found one of the guests from the little soiree. He was sat on a stone bench, looking out into the thick forest. Mountains, forests, and lakes made up about eighty percent of the entire realm, which was probably one of the reasons why it had never boasted a large population.

A light wooden walking stick leaned against the man's leg, and he looked up and me and smiled.

"Gordon," I said.

He got to his feet and hugged me. "Nate, I didn't know you were here," he said before re-taking his seat.

"Tommy roped a few of us in to help with security," I said, settling beside him. "Nice beard," I said. "Distinguished."

"You've grown one too," Gordon said with a smile, stroking his own bushy yet greying beard—being a werewolf certainly had its advantages in the beard-growing department.

I rubbed my short growth. "Laziness," I said with a smile. "How's things?"

"Not too bad," he said. "Hera took London, and I hear you and Mordred fought a dragon, destroying part of the city in the process."

"A small part," I said with a smile. It had been a just over a year since Hera had claimed London as her own, and, if I was honest, it had been a year of peace. I, like many of my friends and allies, was forbidden from returning to London on pain of death, but Hera had needed to spend time getting her stuff sorted, and with Arthur waking from his centuries long coma, it appeared she'd been forced to take a pause and behave. At least for now. It was unlikely to last, but I'd long since learned that you took your good times where you could.

"So, how did Tommy rope you into this?" Gordon asked.

"Ah, he said I needed something to do," I told him. "Apparently, taking some time away from destruction and mayhem is being lazy."

"Considering how much of your life has been destruction and mayhem, maybe he had a point," Gordon said with a smile.

"Well, this is anything but boring." I motioned to the castle. "This whole realm is batshit crazy."

"A hundred years ago, this whole realm was uninhabitable," he said. "I don't know who came up with the idea to turn it into a rich person's getaway, but I'm pretty sure they were rich."

"It must be nice for the people who live here all year around through," I said. "An entire realm for a thousand people for nine months of the year, and only having to put up with people like the wedding party for three months."

"It would be nice if it didn't rain for seven months of the year, and then snow for the rest of it. I think warm days here make up about a week in the year."

"Sounds like Yorkshire," I said, and we both laughed.

"I'm going to tell Matthew you said that," Gordon told me, his smile at the mention of his pack alpha husband, growing wider. "He grew up there."

"Where is Matthew?"

"He likes to go for an evening run before the sun goes down," Gordon said. "The snow gets heavier at night. The runes all around the village and castle make sure we don't wake up with six feet of snow, but out there it'll be different. Matthew didn't know when he'd get the chance for another run."

"You not joining him?" I asked.

"I don't need the run as badly as he does," Gordon said. "Never have. I'm more content to curl up in front of a fire with a good book. Matthew prefers to run until his heart feels like it's going to burst."

We sat in silence for a moment, enjoying the peace.

"How long have you known the bride, or groom, or whichever one it is you know?" I asked, somewhat regretting that I had to break the tranquility.

"Bride," he said. "She's a descendent from the werewolf royalty who signed the pact stopping hostilities with the werelions. The royal family doesn't exist anymore, primarily because everyone just decided to ignore them and go about their business, but it's still a formality that they invite several alphas to their weddings, or funerals, or brunch. Matthew is one of the most powerful alphas in Western Europe, so we get the invite. There are about a dozen of them. Probably the same with the werelions."

"Any chance all of those alphas in one place will cause a problem?"

"Yes, a big one," Gordon said. "But most of them are sensible and don't want trouble. There are one or two who might decide to start a cock measuring exercise, but they're in the minority, and I'm hoping the others will calm anything before it gets out of hand."

"There was an argument brewing in the dining hall," I said. "It's why I left."

Gordon nodded. "The bride's father and the uncle of the groom, I assume," he said with a long sigh. "Both arseholes, I'm afraid. Thankfully, their kids are smarter than them, but they both adhere to the old idea that any slight, imagined or otherwise, must be met with aggression. Matthew can't stand either of them, so I'm guessing by the time we're done, at least one of them is going to get hurt."

"By Matthew?"

Gordon laughed. "No, not unless they try something with him, and that's why Tommy and you guys are here. We both know Tommy is one of the most powerful werewolves in any realm. Everyone respects him because he's earned it. And Diana? Everyone fears her."

"Because they've met her," I said, making Gordon laugh again. "She almost got hit by an apple earlier. Never seen so many people look like they were going to piss themselves."

"Diana might actually be the scariest person I've ever met," Gordon said.

"I'm pretty sure that's why Tommy asked her to come along," I said. "That, and for Remy's amusement."

"Some of the weres don't know what to make of him," Gordon told me.

"They should be wary of him," I said. "He's small, got a big mouth, and is more than happy to back it up."

"How many more of his people did Tommy bring?"

"Twenty-six," I said. "Most of them are in the village getting a feel of the land, talking to the people who work here. This realm has a big security force, so they're trying not to step on any toes, but werewolves and werelions together is not exactly a recipe for a happy time."

"It's all very Shakespearian," Gordon said.

"Remy said the same thing," I told him with a chuckle. "Hopefully, it's less Romeo and Juliet, or Macbeth, and more…" I tried to think of a Shakespearian play that fit the bill. "A Midsummer Night's Dream."

"I'm not entirely sure that any of his plays would make for a fun thing to live through," Gordon said.

"Yeah, I was kind of grasping at straws there," I admitted. "Still, if no one dies, I'll consider this weekend a success."

"How about the loss of a few limbs?" Gordon asked.

I was about to reply when a figure burst out of the forest. He was naked from the waist up, wearing only a pair of denim, knee-length shorts that wouldn't have looked out of place on the

Hulk after he'd turned back into Banner. Matthew was a muscular, hairy man which, seeing how he was a werewolf, wasn't exactly unusual, although he had several dozen scars over his body that he'd gotten before his change. The life of a Knight's Templar had been a hard one for many reasons, most of which Matthew didn't want to talk about.

"Nate," Matthew said, walking over and hugging me.

"You smell like pine needles," I told him.

"I've had an invigorating run," he said as Gordon passed him a red hair tie. Matthew cinched his long, dark hair before kissing his husband on the lips. "I missed you."

"It's been an hour," Gordon said with a wry smile.

Matthew's grin was full of warmth. "Even so, a run with my husband at my side is always preferable to one without."

"Go shower," Gordon said. "You really do smell like pine needles."

Matthew took a deep breath. "I smell of manly smells," he said, which caused Gordon to laugh.

I smiled; it was nice to see them both happy.

"You see how I am treated?" Matthew asked me. "An alpha, and my own husband mocks me."

"Would you prefer if I got someone else to mock you?" Gordon asked.

"Remy isn't busy," I said.

Matthew's eyes narrowed as he looked between us before a deep rumble of laughter burst from him. "I will go shower and change. Can I assume the wedding parties are still at one another's throats?"

I nodded. "I think some of the guests went to explore the realm instead, but basically, yes. It's going to be a long weekend."

Matthew sighed. "I was hoping they would be able to act as adults for a few days."

"To be fair, it was only two of them when I left, although someone came in at the last minute and started shouting at everyone."

"Ah, that would probably be Sven, one of the werelion alphas," Gordon said. "Sven is not known for suffering fools gladly, and he's more interested in keeping the peace than he is in getting into petty squabbles."

"I don't think I've met him," I said.

"He's a good man," Matthew said, which was high praise from a werewolf. "I'm pretty sure Sven and his council are the reason the werelions and wolves haven't gone back to the old ways. He reminds me of Diana a lot. His presence here should stop anyone from thinking about acting in a stupid way."

"Is there a werewolf equivalent here?" I asked.

"The bride's mother, Victoria Walker," Gordon said. "She was one of those who left for a walk. She divorced the father some time ago, and she very much wears the alpha crown without contest. If she'd been there, no one would have started an argument. She'd have thrown them through the damn window."

"I haven't met her either," I said. "Haven't met the bride or groom for that matter."

"Beth and Logan," Gordon said. "Both are sweet kids, although they're about a century old, so the 'kids' thing is subjective. Beth is the spitting image of her mother, in both temperament and looks. Logan is a calm, relaxed, surfer dude type. I'm pretty certain there's never been a situation he couldn't charm himself out of. They're made for one another. A fact Beth's father and Logan's uncle both hate."

"That's why they were fighting," I said.

"Those two have been looking for a fight for a long time," Matthew said. "One killed someone the other liked, or some such. I don't even think either of them know anymore."

There was a shout from deeper in the forest, and all three of us turned to look in the direction.

"Did you see anyone else in there?" I asked Matthew, who shook his head.

I took a step toward the forest when a young woman with dark skin burst out of the dense woodland, stopping a few feet away. She was breathing heavily, her long dark hair sown with leaves. She was completely naked, her body covered in scratches. She looked up at us as if seeing us for the first time, horror in her face, and pitched forward onto the snow, a small crossbow bolt jutting between her shoulder blades.

"Oh shit," Gordon said as he rushed over to her.

"I'll get help," Matthew said, racing off.

I removed my coat and helped Gordon move the woman on to it.

"She's still breathing," Gordon said.

"You know her?" I asked.

Gordon nodded. "It's Victoria, the mother of the bride."

"Oh shit," I whispered as Victoria opened her eyes and screamed.

119

Printed in Poland
by Amazon Fulfillment
Poland Sp. z o.o., Wrocław